W9-BPR-139

GRAND SPRINGS
POLICE DEPARTMENT
ALL POINTS BULLETIN

All officers on call to search for the following:

NAME:	**BRAD IRVING**
Age:	29
Height:	6'0"
Hair:	Dark blond
Eyes:	Dark blue

NAME:	**ANNE PARKER**
Age:	26
Height:	5'5"
Hair:	Light Brown
Eyes:	Green

Last seen New Year's Eve on midnight ski run before avalanche hit. Perhaps have taken shelter in isolated cabin in mountains. May also have been injured.

Special note: These two are ARCH ENEMIES, so watch it—sparks may fly. Approach with extreme caution.

Dear Reader,

The year is ending, and as a special holiday gift to you, we're starting off with a 3-in-1 volume that will have you on the edge of your seat. *Special Report,* by Merline Lovelace, Maggie Price and Debra Cowan, features three connected stories about a plane hijacking and the three couples who find love in such decidedly unusual circumstances. Read it—you won't be sorry.

A YEAR OF LOVING DANGEROUSLY continues with Carla Cassidy's *Strangers When We Married,* a reunion romance with an irresistible baby and a couple who, I know you'll agree, truly do belong together. Then spend 36 HOURS with Doreen Roberts and *A Very...Pregnant New Year's.* This is one family feud that's about to end...at the altar!

Virginia Kantra's back with *Mad Dog and Annie,* a book that's every bit as fascinating as its title—which just happens to be one of my all-time favorite titles. I guarantee you'll enjoy reading about this perfect (though they don't know it yet) pair. Linda Randall Wisdom is back with *Mirror, Mirror,* a good twin/bad twin story with some truly unexpected twists—and a fabulous hero. Finally, read about a woman who has *Everything But a Husband* in Karen Templeton's newest—and keep the tissue box nearby, because your emotions will really be engaged.

And, of course, be sure to come back next month for six more of the most exciting romances around—right here in Silhouette Intimate Moments.

Enjoy!

Leslie J. Wainger
Executive Senior Editor

Please address questions and book requests to:
Silhouette Reader Service
U.S.: 3010 Walden Ave., P.O. Box 1325, Buffalo, NY 14269
Canadian: P.O. Box 609, Fort Erie, Ont. L2A 5X3

A Very...Pregnant New Year's

DOREEN ROBERTS

INTIMATE MOMENTS™

Published by Silhouette Books

America's Publisher of Contemporary Romance

If you purchased this book without a cover you should be aware
that this book is stolen property. It was reported as "unsold and
destroyed" to the publisher, and neither the author nor the
publisher has received any payment for this "stripped book."

Special thanks and acknowledgment are given to
Doreen Roberts for her contribution to the
36 Hours series.

To my husband, Bill. Thank you for giving me a shoulder
to cry on, an arm to lean on and a heart to rely on.
I love you.

 SILHOUETTE BOOKS

ISBN 0-373-27117-4

A VERY...PREGNANT NEW YEAR'S

Copyright © 2000 by Harlequin Books S.A.

All rights reserved. Except for use in any review, the reproduction
or utilization of this work in whole or in part in any form by any
electronic, mechanical or other means, now known or hereafter
invented, including xerography, photocopying and recording, or in
any information storage or retrieval system, is forbidden without
the written permission of the editorial office, Silhouette Books,
300 East 42nd Street, New York, NY 10017 U.S.A.

All characters in this book have no existence outside the imagination of
the author and have no relation whatsoever to anyone bearing the same
name or names. They are not even distantly inspired by any individual
known or unknown to the author, and all incidents are pure invention.

This edition published by arrangement with Harlequin Books S.A.

® and TM are trademarks of Harlequin Books S.A., used under license.
Trademarks indicated with ® are registered in the United States Patent
and Trademark Office, the Canadian Trade Marks Office and in other
countries.

Visit Silhouette at www.eHarlequin.com

Printed in U.S.A.

Books by Doreen Roberts

Silhouette Intimate Moments

Gambler's Gold #215
Willing Accomplice #239
Forbidden Jade #266
Threat of Exposure #295
Desert Heat #319
In the Line of Duty #379
Broken Wings #422
Road to Freedom #442
In a Stranger's Eyes #475
Only a Dream Away #513
Where There's Smoke #567
So Little Time #653
A Cowboy's Heart #705
Every Waking Moment #783
The Mercenary and the
  Marriage Vow #861
*Home Is Where the Cowboy Is #909
*A Forever Kind of Cowboy #927
*The Maverick's Bride #945
A Very...Pregnant New Year's #1047

*Rodeo Men

Silhouette Romance

Home for the Holidays #765
A Mom for Christmas #1195
In Love with the Boss #1271
The Marriage Beat #1380

DOREEN ROBERTS

lives with her husband, who is also her manager and her biggest fan, in the beautiful city of Portland, Oregon. She believes that everyone should have a little adventure now and again to add interest to their lives. She believes in taking risks and has been known to embark on an adventure or two of her own. She is happiest, however, when she is creating stories about the biggest adventure of all—falling in love and learning to live happily ever after.

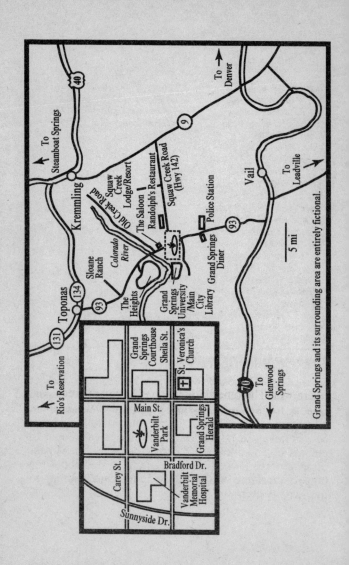

To Denver

40

To Steamboat Springs

9

Kremmling

Squaw Creek Lodge/Resort

Squaw Creek Road (Hwy 142)

Randolph's Restaurant

The Saloon

Old Creek Road

Police Station

Vail

To Leadville

Colorado River

Sloane Ranch

Grand Springs Diner

93

To Toponas

134

131

To Rio's Reservation

93

The Heights

Grand Springs University/Main City Library

5 mi

To Glenwood Springs

70

Grand Springs Courthouse

Sheila St.

St. Veronica's Church

Main St.

Vanderbilt Park

Grand Springs Herald

Carey St.

Bradford Dr.

Vanderbilt Memorial Hospital

Sunnyside Dr.

Grand Springs and its surrounding area are entirely fictional.

Prologue

"Don't touch me!" Anne Parker pushed long, wispy strands of hair out of her eyes and glared at the boy towering over her. She was doing her very best not to cry. After all, she was seven years old. Only babies cried. But she sure felt like crying.

She'd landed in a pile of mushy snow and her pants were wet. The other kids in the schoolyard were staring at her. They made her feel stupid. Worse than that, it was Bradley Irving she'd run into, and he made her feel even more stupid.

He looked down at her and shoved his hands deep into the pockets of his jacket. "I wasn't going to touch you. You can sit there all afternoon for all I care."

"It's all your fault," she said furiously. "You pushed me down."

Bradley scowled at her. "It was your fault. You ran into me."

She frowned back to show him she wasn't afraid, even though her heart banged against her ribs. Bradley had yellow hair and dark blue eyes, and looked like the fierce Viking in her history book. Quickly she looked down at her knee. It was bleeding and had bits of dirt in it. And it hurt.

Her parents had warned her to stay away from Bradley Irving. They called him a delinquent. She wasn't exactly sure what that meant, but it sounded a lot like that picture of the Viking.

When Anne asked questions about Bradley, her parents always said the same thing. He was an Irving and all the Irvings were trouble. In Anne's mind that meant Bradley was mean and could hurt her.

Sometimes she found that hard to understand. He had a really nice face, and once she'd seen him smile at another girl. Seeing him like that had made her feel all warm and squishy inside. Still, her parents were always right and they knew best, as her mother was always telling her. After all, Bradley was ten—almost a teenager. Almost grown-up.

"You'd better get that dirt washed out of there," Bradley said, making her jump. "If you don't, you'll have to get your leg cut off."

His words scared her. Blinking hard, she looked up at him. "You go away, Bradley Irving, and leave me alone. I don't want to talk to you. You're a...a... delinquent!"

His eyes grew darker, and he pushed his chin out, scaring her even more. "And you're a stuck-up spoiled brat. All the Parkers are stuck-up brats."

"I'm not a brat, so there!" Helpless to stop the tears spurting from her eyes, Anne scrambled to her feet. "I hate you, Bradley Irving. I hate you."

"Yeah? Well, I hate you, too, Annie Parker. So that makes us even."

He spun around and marched away from her with his yellow hair flowing in the wind behind him.

Anne watched him go, feeling really bad inside. She didn't really hate him. And she really didn't want him to hate her, either. Confused by feelings she didn't understand, she pulled in her breath to yell her parting shot. "And my name's not Annie. It's Anne—so there!"

The memory of that day haunted Anne throughout her school years. She plagued her mother with endless questions until she'd learned all about the feud between the Irvings and the Parkers. Years ago, Annie May Wilson had left her husband-to-be, Henry Irving, at the altar and had run away to marry John Parker.

Henry Irving had been so angry he'd secretly bought up Parker land and built a spa on it, which made him a wealthy man. The Parkers claimed he'd used a crooked lawyer and had stolen their land. The two families had been fighting over the land ever since.

Anne thought the whole thing terribly romantic, but when she'd said as much to her mother she was forbidden to ever talk about it again. The mere mention of the Irving name, Carol Parker had told her daughter, was enough to give Anne's father a stroke.

During the long, hot summer Anne prepared to attend Burke Senior High, she kept wondering if she'd bump into Brad Irving. The very first week of her freshman year, she saw Brad in the cafeteria, and her heart did a handspring, though she did her best to ignore him. For some silly reason, she kept imagining him in a Viking helmet and carrying a spear. It didn't help matters at all when Emily, her best friend, sighed and called him "dreamy."

When Brad scored the winning touchdown at the Homecoming Game, Anne cheered along with everyone else, though she felt guilty doing it, knowing how her parents would disapprove.

The week before Brad's graduation, Anne missed the bus and had to ride her bike to school. Late for her class, she flew down the hall and around the corner, and crashed straight into a tall, firm body coming the other way. She went down on her knees with her books scattered around her, and knew in that instant that she'd run into more trouble than she could handle.

"Nice block," Brad drawled in his deep voice, "but I should warn you, you're a little late to make the team this year."

Mortified at looking stupid in front of him, she took refuge in anger. She glared up at him and muttered, "It's not my fault if you're dumb enough to get in my way."

The gleam in his dark blue eyes unnerved her. "Well, Miss High-and-Mighty, for that you can pick up your own books."

"Thanks for nothing." She scrambled to her feet and collected her books, praying he would just disappear. This was the closest she'd been to him since grade school, and even a fourteen-year-old recognized a heartbreaker when she saw one. With that sexy smile, awesome body and those dreamy bedroom eyes, it was no wonder the girls hung around him all the time. Not that *she'd* waste her time on him, of course. He was an Irving, after all, and everyone knew what the Irvings were.

"So where's the fire, anyway?"

She lifted her chin. "None of your business."

"I guess you're still a stuck-up brat, Annie Parker."

"I guess you're still a delinquent."

He folded his arms across his broad chest, reminding her again of the childhood Viking image. "Yeah, and all the Parkers are saints."

"We may not be saints, but at least we're not thieves. We don't go around stealing land away from its rightful owners."

"No, you steal wives, instead."

She flipped her hair back over her shoulder with a careless hand. "You can't steal people. Annie Wilson married my great-grandfather because she loved him. It was the Irvings who turned it into a feud when they stole our land."

"We didn't steal the land. That land was bought legally, and it wasn't worth much anyway until my family built the spa on it. Up until then it was just sitting there going to waste."

"It was land that belonged to us, and the Irvings had no right to it. Henry Irving only bought it to get back at John Parker for marrying Annie."

"And you Parkers have been trying to steal it back ever since." His soft, mocking laugh set her teeth on edge. "So what can you do about it, Annie? You're just a stuck-up kid with delusions of grandeur."

"I'd rather be stuck-up than a low-down thief."

Sparks danced in his eyes, but his voice was deceptively quiet when he answered. "Is that right? Well, one day I'll make you and your precious family eat those words, Annie Parker. One by one. See if I don't."

She snorted. "When hell freezes over."

"Watch me."

She watched him disappear around the corner before yelling after him, "And my name's not Annie. It's Anne."

Thank goodness she wouldn't have to worry about him after next week, she told herself, as she stomped down the corridor to her class. Somehow he brought out the worst in her, though she had no idea why she let him get to her like that. She'd heard he was going to college somewhere in the east. With any luck, she'd never see him again.

The years passed swiftly while she followed her fascination with architecture and earned her degree in industrial design. She settled in Denver, and joined a partnership where she began to make a name for herself designing new office complexes.

Her visits home were brief and far between, and although she caught a glimpse of Brad once or twice, she managed to avoid meeting him face-to-face. And if every now and again something prompted a memory of a gorgeous Viking in full battle dress, she quickly erased it from her mind. Brad Irving could drop dead for all she cared.

The night she drove into Grand Springs to spend the holidays with her family, he was the farthest thing from her mind. It wasn't exactly a joyful homecoming. Three months earlier, she'd called off her wedding plans when she'd discovered that her fiancé had spent the night in her chief bridesmaid's bed.

Devastated by the betrayal, she'd given up her apartment, as well as her life in Denver, and was coming home to lick her wounds. There were worse places to make a living than Grand Springs, she'd decided. The town had grown in the four years she'd been gone, she could make use of her talents. And it would be good to be home, at least for a while.

Dan and Carol Parker welcomed their wounded daughter with open arms and undisguised sympathy. Her brother, Paul, pointed out how much better off she was without the jerk, while Sharon and Elise, her younger sisters, assured her there were plenty more apples in the orchard.

Anne had no intention of getting involved with another man. Ever. Convinced that all men were scum, she had no trouble adding Bradley Irving to that list when her sisters filled her in on the latest gossip.

Eighteen years had gone by since the last confrontation in high school. Brad now had a successful law practice right there in Grand Springs, and was gaining a reputation as the town's most eligible bachelor. Since his father had died two years earlier, leaving Brad sole heir to his estate, this came as no surprise to Anne. He might be an Irving, but there was no denying Brad was devastating to look at. That combination of money and looks would be enough to draw the women like flies to a garbage can.

According to her sisters, Brad's conquests were numerous and well publicized. That, and the fact that he was in his thirties and still single only confirmed Anne's opinion of him. Brad Irving was a no-good womanizer with the manners of a barbarian. No better than a Viking savage.

When Anne discovered that her father had arranged to take the family to Mountview Ski Lodge for the New Year weekend celebrations, she did her best to get out of the popular social event. She just wasn't in the mood for partying. The combined efforts of her parents, sisters and brother failed to change her mind, but when James Parker put in his own plea, she found it impossible to refuse her beloved grandfather.

On the night she reluctantly checked into the lodge, she was determined to make the best of things for the sake of her family.

After settling into her room, she hurried down the wide stairs to join her family in the dining room for dinner. As she rounded the corner of the crowded lobby, she ran smack into someone coming the other way.

With a surprised yelp, she bounced off the man's muscular body and hit the wall hard with her shoulder. The impact jolted her purse out of her hand and it skidded across the polished floor between the feet of two young women who had just entered the lodge.

Anne didn't need to look at the man she'd collided with to recognize him. She'd have known that deep, mocking voice anywhere.

"Are you always this clumsy, Annie Parker, or is this just your way of getting my attention?"

Anne gritted her teeth. It seemed she was destined to spend her life crashing into Brad Irving.

Chapter 1

Embarrassed, Anne retrieved her purse from the two grinning young women, then turned to face the man who seemed determined to make a fool of her.

He towered over her, like some awful instance of déjà vu, with just a hint of amusement in his expression. His hair looked darker than she remembered—more gold than yellow—and curled almost to his collar.

Determined not to let him destroy her composure, she decided that to attack was her best defense. "Well, if it isn't the delinquent," she murmured. "I'm surprised to see you. I would have thought a town like Grand Springs would have cramped your style by now."

"Ah, that's just where you're wrong. Grand Springs still holds plenty of opportunities for an enterprising young man or woman with ambition."

"So I heard," Anne said dryly.

He gave her an audacious grin. Against her will, she noticed how well his creamy white sweater emphasized his broad shoulders, and how closely his black wool slacks skimmed his hips in a perfect fit. Brad Irving had grown up. And he was still drop-dead gorgeous. No wonder the women were falling all over him. If she'd known he was going to be at the lodge, she told herself fiercely, she definitely would have stayed at home.

"Rumor has it that you're thinking about coming back here to live," Brad said casually. "Big city life got to be too much for you?"

She shrugged, wondering how much he'd heard on the small town grapevine. "Something like that."

"You'll find the town has grown quite a bit since you left. Let me know if you need some pointers on the hot spots. I'm always available for advice and assistance."

Annoyed at the way her pulse had jumped, Anne said cooly, "Thanks. I'm sure you're an expert on the subject but I'm not interested in the nightlife of Grand Springs right now."

She didn't like the gleam in his eye when he answered her. "I was talking about apartments, places of business, that kind of thing."

Again, he'd managed to make her feel foolish. "I think I can find my way around."

"Well, the offer's always there."

She wasn't about to be added to his list of conquests, she vowed silently. "I'm sure you have better things to do than entertain a Parker. Unless you're figuring on starting World War III."

He shook his head. "I decided a long time ago to stay neutral as far as the Irving versus Parker feud is concerned. All that pent-up hostility and backstabbing takes up too much energy."

She suspected he was making fun of her family, but wasn't sure enough to call him on it. Anxious to escape the magnetism of that killer smile, she said cooly, "Well, I have to run." Good manners nudged her to say something conventional, such as how nice it was to see him again. She smothered the urge and turned to leave, just as the clatter of high heels echoed across the spacious dark-paneled lobby.

"Really, Brad," a husky voice exclaimed, "can't you find something better to do than hang around the lobby all evening?"

Brad's face seemed to close up. "I was just on my way in to dinner, Mother."

With a great deal of reluctance, Anne paused to acknowledge the woman standing behind her.

Darlene Irving was not a tall woman, but what she lacked in height she made up for in flamboyance. Taste had never been one of Darlene's attributes. Her long, tight black skirt was slit up to her thigh, and she'd teamed it with a low-cut red halter top that revealed more of her uplifted bosom than Anne cared to see. Obviously Darlene had not lost her fondness for exploiting her generous figure. Her bleached platinum hair was drawn back in a tight knot at the back of her head, which displayed her cheekbones but emphasized the deep wrinkles in her neck.

Darlene looked like an aging hooker, Anne thought, and immediately chastised herself. "Good evening, Mrs. Irving," she murmured, wishing she'd simply pretended not to notice the woman.

Darlene patted her immaculate hair, allowing Anne to see the flash of light explode from the large square-cut diamond on her right hand. "Oh, it's you, Annie."

Anne pursed her lips. "I prefer to be called Anne."

"Really." Darlene looked momentarily taken aback, but instantly recovered. "I heard all about your unfortunate experience, you poor dear. Fancy being dumped practically at the altar like that. Must have been devastating for you. Men can be such arrogant beasts. I suppose some people might say it was poetic justice, considering what happened to poor Henry Irving, but of course I wouldn't dream of making such an assumption."

"Mother—"

Brad's muttered protest was ignored as Darlene rushed on. "One has to be so careful whom they trust in a big city. So many weirdos. And all that pollution! Such an aging effect on one. You look positively worn out, Annie. I heard you were painting office buildings now."

Anne placed a smile on her face. At least Brad had the decency to look uncomfortable, she noticed. Wondering why she was bothering to defend herself against this obnoxious woman, she said deliberately, "Not painting. Designing. I'm an architect."

"Really." Darlene looked as if she'd just smelled something bad. "How terribly quaint." She reached out a manicured hand and patted Brad on the shoulder. "You hear that, Brad? An architect. It's really amazing what they allow women to do nowadays."

She gave Anne the kind of look a cat gives when it's brought home a dead mouse. "Brad's law firm is doing very well, you know."

Brad shrugged, looking embarrassed, as well he might.

"Well, good for him." Anne kept her icy gaze on Darlene's face. "You must be so proud of him."

"I am. He's been such a comfort since poor Wally died."

Remembering her manners, Anne swallowed her temper and said quietly, "I'm so sorry to hear about the loss of your husband. It must be very hard for you."

Darlene sighed. "Yes, it is. One tends to lean on family at times like these."

"Speaking of which," Anne said, grasping the opportunity, "I'm supposed to be at the dinner table right now with my family."

Darlene's heavily painted face took on a look of dismay. "Your family is here, too?"

"The entire family," Anne assured her with ill-concealed satisfaction. "My parents, my brother and sisters, as well as my grandfather are all here to celebrate the new year."

"Good heavens," Darlene murmured. "The whole clan. I had no idea." She turned to her son, her oversized, gold earrings swinging an inch or two above her shoulders. "Well, Brad darling, I suppose we shall just have to make the best of it. No doubt we'll be falling over Parkers all weekend."

Anne had finally had enough. With a muttered "Excuse me," she turned her back on them and headed for the dining room. Revolting woman, she thought, seething with indignation. Anyone would think the holiday celebration had been planned entirely for her benefit, and that the Parkers were irritating intruders. Brad might have declared his neutrality, but his mother obviously intended to keep the Irving banner flying.

Her encounter had robbed her of an appetite, but she was not about to let anyone know that. Nor was she about to let the insufferable Irvings ruin the weekend. She would simply have to do her level best to avoid them.

Brad watched Anne disappear through the main doors of the dining room, feeling more than a little sorry for her. She'd met her match when dueling with his mother's acid tongue. Though he had to admire the way she'd hung on to her composure. The fourteen-year-old kid he remembered would have instantly retaliated with a barrage of insults.

Remembering that last encounter in the halls of Burke Senior High, he twisted his mouth in a wry smile. He kind of missed that hot-tempered, spunky attitude of hers. Though her green eyes still sparkled with fire when she was mad.

"Pretentious little brat," Darlene sputtered. "Did you see the way she looked at me? *I prefer to be called Anne.* The Parkers think they're all so superior. Not that *she* has anything to preen about. Little wonder her boyfriend dumped her at the altar, if she patronized him the way she does everyone else. She deserves what she gets, that's what I say."

"Mother," Brad said mildly, "I'm really not interested in anything that is remotely connected to the Parkers, so why don't we just change the subject.''

Darlene sniffed. ''Well, you should be. It was the Parkers who put your father into an early grave.''

He felt the familiar stab of pain at the mention of his dad, and he made an effort to keep his tone even, ''Dad died because his heart couldn't handle the stress of running the resort. You know that as well as I do.''

''He died,'' Darlene said deliberately, ''because he killed himself trying to hold on to that stupid piece of property rather than allow it to be sold back to the Parkers. He'd turn over in his grave if he knew it was shut down.''

''The Coldwater Spa was operating at a loss for the last few years. It was just a matter of time before he closed it down.''

''The right person could have made it profitable again.''

He knew what she was getting at, and he knew where that topic would lead. He'd fought with his father often enough over his decision to go to law school instead of taking over the management of the resort. He wasn't about to fight with his mother over it, too.

''Well, it's closed down now,'' he said cheerfully, ''so let's just stop worrying about it and enjoy this weekend.''

He might have known she wouldn't let it go that easily.

''If your father hadn't stipulated in his will that the land had to stay in the family,'' Darlene said, as they crossed the lobby together, ''we could have asked a good price for Coldwater and been rid of it. If it hadn't been for the Parkers and that ridiculous feud, we wouldn't be stuck with it.''

"You can't blame everything on the Parkers." Brad paused at the entrance to the dining room. "We'll enjoy the weekend a lot more if you just forget about the feud *and* the Parkers. Pretend they're not here."

Darlene sniffed. "That's going to be a little difficult considering the entire mob is here. I don't know how you can be so calm about it. After all, if it hadn't been for that family, you would probably have had a better relationship with your father."

Brad winced. It was a low blow, and there was just no answer to that. Wishing he were anywhere else but at Mountview Ski Lodge that weekend, he escorted his mother into the dining room.

A few yards away, Anne sat at a long table at the far end of the room, next to one of the tall windows overlooking the slopes. She'd always loved the rustic atmosphere of the lodge, with its wide, natural beams and cathedral ceilings. Logs crackled and spat in the huge stone fireplace just feet away, and she could feel the heat from the hungry flames as she looked around the table at her family.

It was so good to be with them all again, though she missed her grandma Nellie. She smiled at Grandpa James, who sat next to her. She couldn't resist giving him a hug. "How are you doing, Grandpa?"

His pale gray eyes peered at her over the top of his

glasses. "I'd feel a damn sight better if it was colder."

She was immediately concerned. "Are you too hot? Would you like to move? I'm sure they'll be happy to set up another table further away from the fire."

He shook his head. "I'm fine. It's the snow I'm worried about." He nodded at the window. "Looks a little mushy to me."

Paul, who was sitting on the other side of him, gave him a nudge with his elbow. "You planning on skiing with us, Gramps?"

Grandpa James shook his head. "Got too much respect for my old bones." He gave Paul a stern look. "Stay off that mountain, sonny, if you value your skin." He glanced around the table. "That goes for all of you. Not safe out there. Temperature's rising. Take my word for it."

Paul laughed. At twenty-four he was a carbon copy of their father, except his dark blond hair showed no signs of the thinning that plagued Dan Parker. Paul had inherited his father's broad shoulders and chunky build, and was supremely confident of his immortality. "You worry too much, Gramps. We're all fantastic skiers. After all, we've been doing it since we were old enough to walk."

Grandpa scowled at him. "Don't mess with Mother Nature, boy. You'll find out she has a mean hand."

"Oh, for heaven's sake, Father, stop treating them all as if they were still toddlers." Carol Parker, an attractive woman from whom Anne had inherited her thick hair and green eyes, gazed fondly at her four children. "Though sometimes I have to admit, it's hard for me to realize you are all so grown-up. Especially now that we're all together again.'' She reached out and lightly pressed Anne's hand. ''I'm so glad you're coming back to Grand Springs, darling. We've missed you.''

''I've missed you all, too.'' Anne sipped at her iced tea before adding casually, ''I bumped into the Irvings in the foyer.''

Her father groaned. ''Oh, no, don't tell me that awful woman is here. You didn't speak to her, did you? She gives the place a bad name. I suppose she's got that scheming son of hers with her? She never goes anywhere without him now that Wally's gone.''

''Now, Dan, let's not let those dreadful people spoil our weekend.'' Carol looked hopefully at Anne for support. ''The best thing to do is completely ignore them. Pretend we don't see them.''

''I couldn't agree more.'' Secretly Anne thought that might be impossible, considering the lodge wasn't that big.

''Well, I'm glad Brad Irving's here,'' Sharon said, smirking at Elise. ''I think he's positively awesome looking.''

''The sexiest man in town, that's for sure.'' Elise flicked her long blond hair over her shoulder with a careless hand. ''I wouldn't mind spending a night with him, I can tell you.''

''That's enough, girls,'' Carol warned mildly. ''You know how talk like that irritates your father.''

''The man's a damn crook,'' Dan muttered. ''How can you two talk like that about a man whose family stole your heritage? If it wasn't for the Irvings, we'd still own that damn land, and I wouldn't have to face bankruptcy to keep you two in college.''

Sharon's face burned as she reached for her water glass. Elise lifted her chin, and Anne knew her youngest sister was going to argue. She should have kept her mouth shut about seeing Brad and his mother, she thought, cursing herself for starting a familiar argument.

''Well, it's not worth much now,'' Elise said, with a hint of defiance. ''Now that they've closed down the spa it's just empty buildings sitting there doing nothing.''

''It's still good land.'' Dan set his fork down on his plate with a clatter. ''I'm damn sure I could find something to do with it. Trust that thieving lawyer to let it go to waste. Too damn busy cheating people out of their hard-earned money, that's his problem.''

''Now, dear, let's just forget about it, shall we?'' Carol looked pleadingly at her husband. ''I really would like to enjoy this weekend with my wonderful family, and for once forget the existence of the Irvings.''

''That's not going to be easy,'' Sharon said, echoing Anne's thoughts. ''Brad will be on the midnight ski run. There's only fifteen of us signed up, so we're bound to bump into him.''

''Cool,'' Elise murmured softly, earning a frown from her father.

''We signed you up for it, Anne,'' Sharon said eagerly. ''Paul's going, too. It should be fun. I love skiing at night.''

So did Anne, but the thought of racing down a dark mountain next to Brad Irving took the joy out of it.

She smiled at her sisters. "I think I'll pass. It's been a while since I was on skis."

"I think you should all pass it up," Grandpa James muttered. "You're all crazy if you go down that mountain."

"You've got to go, Anne!" Elise cried in dismay. "It won't be the same without you. There's going to be a welcome-back party for the skiers and everything."

"Not afraid of Brad Irving, are you?" Sharon asked slyly.

Anne felt her cheeks grow warm. "Of course not," she said sharply. "If you really want me to go that badly, I'll go."

Grandpa James shook his head. "Crazy," he muttered. "Every last one of them."

"We're bound to see Brad at the New Year's Eve party, anyway," Paul said, eyeing the huge tray of desserts placed on the table by an attractive waitress. "So we might as well meet the enemy on the slopes and beat the heck out of him."

Carol looked alarmed. "You're not going to fight that man, are you Paul? I despise the Irvings as much as anyone, but I wouldn't want to see you fight."

Paul grinned. "Relax, Mom. I just meant we'd all beat him down the mountain, that's all."

"That's if you get down," Grandpa muttered darkly.

Aware that no one was listening to him, as usual, Anne patted his arm. "Don't worry, Grandpa," she said softly. "I'll keep an eye on them all."

"Tell us about your plans for the new year, Anne dear." Carol picked up a dish of cheesecake and offered it to her eldest daughter. "I'm dying to know what you intend to do next."

"I thought I'd find an office to rent downtown," Anne said, doing her best not to notice Brad and his mother seated at the opposite end of the room. Elise and Sharon might think that Bradley Irving was the sexiest man in town, she told herself, but personally, she couldn't see it.

Trust Darlene Irving to mention her aborted wedding. The thought of Jason didn't enter her mind anymore until someone mentioned him. Actually, compared to the suave, confident man across the room, Jason was a wimp.

The thought surprised her. She hastily reminded herself that, wimp or not, Brad Irving was just as much a womanizer as Jason, and infinitely more irritating. Then she deliberately put them both out of her mind for the rest of the meal.

By late afternoon the following day, the clouds that had been gathering all afternoon had gradually thickened to a thick gray mass above the slopes. By the time Anne and her siblings joined the midnight skiers at the chairlifts, the wind danced through the branches of the pines and tossed mounds of snow to the ground below. A fine mist hung over the lodge, obliterating the night sky.

Grandpa James had already retired for the night, but Dan and Carol had settled themselves by the fire to await the return of their family.

Elise and Sharon chattered endlessly as they waited for their turn on the lifts. Standing behind them, Anne listened to Paul's account of his work as a computer analyst without really understanding what he was talking about. Her attention was on a tall, blond man at the rear of the line, deep in conversation with a redhead who laughed at everything he said. Anne wondered if they were at the lodge together, then told herself it was none of her business. Though she did wonder how romantic a rendezvous could be if Brad had brought his mother along.

Some of the guests had braved the cool night wind to cheer on the skiers, and would remain on the terrace to watch the descent. The team's headlamps would provide a pleasing display of bobbing lights as they swooped down the mountain.

Anne clasped her ski poles as she stepped onto the line next to Paul and waited for the chair to swing in behind them. Tiny flakes of snow drifted down in the flare of the lights and danced now and again in a flurry of wind.

The faint smell of pine perfumed the clean night air, and Anne felt a stirring of anticipation as the edge of the chair closed in behind her knees. She settled herself on the seat, prepared to enjoy the ride to the top of the run. This was the part she loved—the moments before she launched herself into the wild, exhilarating journey down the still, silent world of the slopes.

She had never lost her thrill of the run—that rush of heady excitement as her skis swished through the smooth, white snow and the cold wind whipped her face. For a few brief minutes she could leave behind all the worries and stress of her workday world, and transcend to a calmer, more peaceful place where all that mattered was the frosty ground slipping away beneath her feet as she sped on wings to the earth below.

"The snow's coming down pretty good," Paul remarked, as they reached the end of their ride and slid gracefully from their chair. "If those clouds get any lower they won't see our lights from the lodge."

Anne glanced up at the black sky above her. "We should be down before the worst of the storm comes in."

"I see our hotshot lawyer has found himself another candidate for heartbreak," Paul muttered.

She followed his gaze to where Brad was helping the redhead out of the chair. The woman fell against him and he caught her, wrapping his arms around her to steady her. Anne watched her laugh up at him, clinging to him as if she were helpless to stand by herself. Heaven knew what the silly woman would do once she got on the slopes, Anne thought.

She tried to ignore the two of them as she took her place at the top of the run. Paul and his sisters lined up on her left, and she was relieved to see Brad and his giggling girlfriend at the opposite end of the line.

Their leader stood in the middle of the group, ready to lead off on his own. After a count of five, the person on each side of him would follow, then the person on each side of them, until all fifteen skiers were descending in a giant V formation.

Anne forgot about Brad as she poised on her mark, waiting for her turn. With a shout that echoed across the still mountain, the lead took off, disappearing into the eerie half darkness. Within seconds the beam of his flashlight sliced through the falling snow, which was the signal for the next two to go, then the next.

Anne waited for the flash of light to signal her turn, then launched herself forward. Her spirits soared as her skis cut through the snow, and she crouched to gain speed. Ahead of her the bobbing lights of the skiers guided her down a trail that was hard to see against the blowing snow. Thick flakes slanted across the wide beam of her headlamp, bringing her visibility down to a few feet ahead of her.

A quick glance back assured her that Paul and her sisters were close behind her, though it was impossible to distinguish their faces in the dark. She faced forward again, and as she did so, a loud crack echoed across the mountainside, followed by an ominous rumbling.

At first she thought it was thunder, but when the sound grew louder instead of fading away, she flicked a glance over her shoulder. Faintly she heard Paul's shout above the ever increasing roar, but she couldn't understand what he said. The next time she looked back he waved his arm frantically up and down. Her apprehension leapt to alarm when she saw her two sisters veer off sharply to their left.

Then the significance of the thundering roar hit her, and her heart seemed to freeze in fear. Just a few yards behind Paul, barely distinguishable in the dim light, a wall of snow loomed above him, bearing down on him fast.

Avalanche. The thing every mountain skier and climber dreaded. The tumbling, suffocating mass of snow and debris was hurtling down on the skiers, with the lodge itself directly in its path.

Instinctively, Anne dug in her poles and leaned to her left, beginning the curve that would take her out of the path of the deadly flow. One frantic glance back assured her that her sisters had reached the trees and were clear of the onslaught. Seconds later she saw Paul plunge after them, barely escaping the edge of the swirling, heaving mass of destruction.

The furious white wave was almost on her now, like a giant breaker in the rolling surf. The noise was deafening. Twenty yards. She dug her poles frantically into the soft snow, desperate for more speed.

Almost there. She could see the edge of the trees, then suddenly lost sight of them as a cloud of wet snow enveloped her. The freezing air closed around her, choking her, blinding her. She fought to keep her balance as she felt the ground shift beneath her. Then something hit her hard in the shoulder.

She went flying, rolling and tumbling at a terrifying speed inside the cold, wet suffocating blanket of snow. Just when she thought she would never draw breath again, the ground abruptly gave way beneath her.

Barely conscious now, she realized she was falling. Her last thought was to wonder how long it would take for her grieving family to find her body at the bottom of a ravine. Then the darkness wiped out the world.

Chapter 2

At the first faint rumble of thunder, the spectators on the terrace looked expectantly up toward the mountain peaks. They could see nothing through the driving snow. Not even the skiers' lights. Some of them grumbled that it wasn't worth waiting outside in the cold.

Only a handful stayed behind to witness the awesome sight of what seemed to be half the mountain bearing down on the lodge. Screaming warnings, the guests scattered and raced for shelter. Seconds later the terrace was torn from its supports, and the formidable roar of the avalanche swallowed up the splintering sound of shattered windows.

In his room on the second floor, Dr. Tony Petrocelli paused in the act of removing his shirt and tilted his dark head to one side. The noise he heard sounded like a freight train coming out of a tunnel. He frowned at his wife, who sat on the edge of the bed, staring up at him with anxious blue eyes.

"What is it?" Beth asked, her voice a mere whisper.

Tony shrugged. "Beats me. Probably some kind of celebration—" He broke off, his words cut off by the sound of splintering wood and groaning timbers.

Beth's eyes grew round. "What's happening?"

"I don't know," Tony said grimly. "But I think we'd better find out." He grabbed his wife's jacket off the back of the chair and threw it to her. "I have a feeling you're going to need this."

On her feet in an instant, Beth shrugged her arms into the parka. "Thank God we left Christopher with your family," she muttered as she followed her husband out the door.

Downstairs by the fireplace, Carol Parker thought she was imagining things as she stared at the snow piling up through the jagged remains of the windows. She turned to Dan, who looked as horrified as she felt. "The kids," she said urgently. "What happened to our kids?"

Dan wrapped his arms around her. "Don't worry, they'll be fine."

She heard the forced assurance in his voice and her blood chilled. "Dan, they were on the mountain. They were all on the mountain." Her voice rose as she struggled to free herself from his hold. "Dear God, Dan, where are they?"

Everything seemed to be a blur after that. She heard Dan's voice, trying to calm her, but she was incapable of thinking clearly. People seemed to be everywhere, some rushing about, some sitting, some lying still on

the floor. She saw Darlene Irving, crying and screaming, while a woman with auburn hair tried to comfort
her. Recognizing Beth Petrocelli, Carol felt a moment's relief that her husband would be somewhere
around as well. Tony Petrocelli was a good doctor,
and it looked as if some of those people would need
his help.

She thought about the girls and Paul, lying injured
out there somewhere, helpless and alone. The agonized groan she heard was her own.

Dan's hands tightened on her shoulders and he
gave her a little shake. "Snap out of it, Carol. I have
to go outside and help dig out the people buried under
the debris. I need you to stay with Dad. He's insisting
on helping and I don't want him out there. Get it
together, Carol. I need you."

Her mind cleared, and she stared at him, her feeling
of dread threatening to overwhelm her. "We have to
find them, Dan," she whispered.

His blue eyes stared back at her, and she found
strength in the resolution she saw in them. "Doc Petrocelli is organizing a search party. As soon as it's
light I'll go with them, and I won't come back without the kids. Will you be okay here now?"

She nodded and managed a stiff smile. "Just be
careful out there. That snow is treacherous."

"Try not to worry. Just help out here where you
can."

It was easier to be busy, she realized, as she herded
Grandpa into the dining room where several people
sat propped against the wall. The opposite wall had
caved in with the weight of the snow, but the roof

was still intact. Obviously the worst of the avalanche had missed the lodge.

Obeying Beth Petrocelli's instructions, she helped clean grazes and cuts and apply bandages. Grandpa, having accepted the fact that he would be more hindrance than help, was doing his best to cheer up the wounded with his ancient jokes.

According to the comments Carol overheard, half the lodge was buried beneath the weight of the snow, and the avalanche had completely cut off the road to town. Dr. Petrocelli would have his hands full until help arrived.

When Paul suddenly popped up in front of Carol, she let out a shriek of joy. When she saw Sharon and Elise behind him, she burst into tears. Swept up in her relief, it was a moment or two before she realized that her eldest daughter was not with them.

Struggling to keep the panic at bay, she clung to Paul's arm. "Anne," she said urgently. "Where is she?"

She knew at once by the agony on Paul's face that she didn't want to hear what he had to tell her.

"She was right on the edge of it, Mom," he said, his voice shaky. "I'm sure she'll be okay. Dad and I will be joining the search party as soon as it's light. We'll find her. I know we will."

Her fingers tightened as she heard her daughters begin to cry. She had to be strong. For their sakes, she had to be strong. Paul was right. He and Dan would find her baby. They just had to find her.

Hold on, my precious daughter, she urged silently. *Just please, hold on.*

* * *

It was cold. So incredibly cold, and something wet
and heavy pressed down on her head. The wall supporting her back felt like a jagged block of ice. Her
right leg was jammed up against something hard that
barely shifted when she tried to move it.

Darkness enveloped her like a thick black blanket.
She couldn't see anything at all. For a moment she
panicked, wondering if she was blind. She shook her
head, trying to clear her fogged mind. Pain sliced
across her eyes and she moaned.

Her wool hat, headlamp and goggles were gone,
and whatever was sitting on top of her head slid down
with a plop onto her lap. Some of it seeped into her
collar, freezing her neck.

Snow. Now she remembered.

Cautiously she tilted her head back. Above her she
could see a patch of light gray. Nothing else. But at
least she could see. Feeling a little better, she moved
her hand and felt the cold, hard ground beneath her.
She stretched her arm to explore a little farther, and
her nerves received a nasty jolt when her fingers en-
countered thin air. Patting the ground on either side
of her, she faced the truth. She was on a ledge. A
very narrow ledge.

The pungent smell of pine told her that the thing
pressing against her right leg was a broken tree. She
clung to it for a moment, aware that it had probably
saved her life. So far, anyway.

Her spirits plummeted as the reality of her predic-
ament dawned on her. She had fallen into a ravine.
By a miracle she'd landed on a ledge. She was alive,
and except for a bad headache and an excruciating

pain in her right ankle, she apparently had no serious injuries. That was the good news.

The bad news was that it would be next to impossible to climb out of there. Even if she could find a slight foothold in the sheer face of the wall behind her, her experimental wiggling of her right foot told her she'd either broken or sprained her ankle. The ledge was so narrow she was frightened to move. One slip and she could plummet anywhere from a few yards to several hundred feet, depending on the depth of the ravine. That was something she wouldn't know until it was light enough to see. If she lived that long in this bitter cold.

For several minutes depression and panic overwhelmed her. She began yelling with all the breath she could muster, even though she had little hope of anyone hearing her. She yelled until she was exhausted, and finally her breath died on a sob. It was no good. She was going to die there, alone on the mountain.

She started thinking about her family, and how they must be feeling. She struggled to remember those last terrifying moments, and felt sure that Paul and her sisters had jumped clear of the avalanche's fury. She wondered if the snow had covered the lodge, and if everyone there was all right. What if they'd all been buried? Her grandfather, her parents…what would Elise and Sharon do without them? Paul could take care of himself, but her sisters would be devastated.

A cold, wet tear slid slowly down her cheek, and she dashed it away with the back of her hand. She had to pull herself together. If she was going to die, she refused to go whimpering like a baby, she thought fiercely. She shifted her position, trying to get more comfortable, and realized one of her skis was still attached to her injured foot. The other must have come off in her wild tumble through the snow.

She couldn't reach her foot to take off the ski, and she couldn't pull her foot toward her because the ski was jammed behind the tree. She slumped back against the wall, fighting against the return of panic. In her entire life, she'd never felt so alone.

She thought about her grandfather, and tried to guess what he would tell her now. All her life she'd gone to him for advice, from the time when she was six and her parents wouldn't let her have a puppy until four years ago when she'd wrestled with her decision to live in Denver. Somehow Grandpa James was easier to talk to than her parents, much as she loved them. Grandpa had a way of really listening to her, and never judged her—never laughed at her silly notions the way her father sometimes did.

She closed her eyes and imagined he was there with her, sitting by her side, listening to her woes. After a while she heard his gravelly voice, as clearly as if he'd spoken to her. *Sing,* he told her. *Singing lifts the spirits. Make as much noise as you can. Sing your heart out, Anne. Sing!*

She sang. Every song she could think of. And when she didn't know the words she made them up. She was in the middle of a rousing chorus of "God Bless America" when a faint sound penetrated her high-pitched screeching.

She snapped her mouth shut and held her breath. If there was a timber wolf out there she didn't want to let it know that its next meal was just a few feet away. In the silence that followed she thought she must have imagined the noise, and gathered her breath to blast out another chorus. Before she could let it out, however, she heard the noise again. Closer this time.

Excitement gripped her as she strained her ears. She was either suffering from delusion, or that was a human voice she'd heard. Tears welled up and ran unchecked down her cheeks when she heard the shout again. It *was* a human voice. And he wasn't too far away.

Terrified that he'd pass right by her, she dragged in her breath and let it out in a furious bellow of desperation. "Help! Please help me!"

"Hang on, I'm coming. Just keep yelling."

"I'm down here, in a ravine. Please, be careful." The last thing she needed was a man's heavy body tumbling down on top of her. More than likely he'd send them both hurtling to their deaths.

She refused to think about that, but waited in an agony of suspense until she heard another shout. It was much closer this time.

"Where are you?"

"Wait! Don't move. You're close to the edge of the ravine. Wait a minute and I'll send up a snowball." She quickly gathered up some snow and formed it into a ball. "Are you ready?"

"Yes, throw away!"

His voice sounded muffled, and vaguely familiar. Excited now, she braced herself against the wall. She would have to throw underarm…she had no room to bring her elbow back for an overarm throw. Praying she had the strength to lob the snowball high enough for her rescuer to see it, she leaned forward and flung her hand skyward.

The snowball shot out of her hand and she saw it silhouetted against the gray patch of sky, then it fell like a stone. She never heard it land. She tried not to think how far down it had fallen.

She peered up at the gray patch and yelled, "Did you see it?"

"I saw it." Seconds later a beam of light flashed downward, blinding her. "I have to tell you, Annie Parker, that was the worst rendition of "God Bless America" I've ever heard."

She blinked, her mind refusing to accept what her ears had heard. It couldn't be. She was imagining things again.

Then he spoke again, chasing away any doubt in her mind. "I know how you big city dwellers crave excitement, but isn't this going a little too far?"

She groaned aloud. Unbelievable. A whole damn mountain out there and Brad Irving had to be the one to stumble across her. In the next instant she was ashamed of her uncharitable thought. She could have died in that ravine if he hadn't found her.

Concern crept into his voice as he peered down at her. "Are you hurt?"

His face looked ghostly in the reflection from his headlamp, but there was no mistaking those chiseled features. She roused herself to answer. "My ankle hurts, but otherwise I'm okay."

"Is it broken?"

She wiggled it and winced. "I don't think so. But my foot is jammed behind this broken tree and I can't get my ski off."

The light moved off her face and probed around her. For the first time she could see the edge of the ledge and the blackness beyond. Her stomach heaved. She had less room than she thought. She watched the headlamp's beam move over the broken tree and her shattered ski.

"Looks like we'll have to shift that tree before we can get you up," Brad said, with a lot more confidence than the situation warranted, in Anne's opinion.

"I might go down with it," she said, her voice trembling.

"Suit yourself, but I don't recommend it."

His cheerful tone irritated her. The last thing she needed right now was his warped sense of humor. "So what do you suggest? That's if you're capable of coming up with a practical solution."

"If I don't, then I guess you're stuck down there. If I were you I'd think about that, Annie, and try to be civil to me."

Deciding to play it safe, she said dryly, "I'll do my best, but my temperament is not at its greatest right now. For reasons you should be able to understand. And by the way, since you seem to keep forgetting, the name's Anne."

"Right."

The light disappeared, leaving her in the cold darkness once more. She looked up, but all she could see was the patch of gray above her. For a terrifying moment of disbelief she thought he'd left her, but then the beam slashed across her face again, temporarily blinding her.

She could hear Brad grunting and cursing, and a

shower of snow descended on her, then she saw his face suspended above her again.

"Can't shift the tree from up here," he said, sounding breathless. "You'll have to try and shove it away from you at your end."

"I don't think I can," she said miserably.

"You can if I'm hanging on to you. I think I can reach you from here. Stretch your arms up and see if you can reach my hands."

She saw his gloved hands sliding down toward her. He had to be lying flat on his stomach in the snow. She stretched as high as she could. There was at least a six-inch gap between her fingers and his. "Not without standing up," she said, trying not to let defeat creep into her voice.

"Okay, hang on." Again he disappeared, and she waited, feeling the cold gnawing at her bones. Seconds later something slithered over the edge and snaked down toward her.

"Buckle this belt around one of your wrists," Brad ordered. "I've got the other end around mine. It will hold you while you kick the tree out from the ledge."

She took off one of her gloves long enough to fasten the belt around her wrist, then pulled it on again. "Okay, I'm ready."

"Before we do this," Brad said calmly, "I should tell you I don't have a lot of traction up here. So try not to fall off the ledge, okay?"

She understood what he meant. The avalanche had laid a blanket of deep, soft snow over the area. It would be slippery even to walk on. Trying to get traction in it would be almost impossible. There was every chance that in trying to get her out of there,

Brad could very well fall down in there with her. She didn't want to think about where they might end up.

"Look," she said, with just a slight waver in her voice. "Are you sure about this? I mean, I could wait here while you go get help."

"We don't have time for that. I've lost my skis and it could take hours, if not days, to get down the mountain on foot, even if I could find my way. It's snowing like crazy up here."

She could tell that from the snowflakes drifting down on her face. He was right, she didn't have that much time. Already she could feel the numbness creeping up her right leg. "Okay," she said unsteadily. "Let's do it."

"Right. I've got a good hold on you, so I want you to kick that tree out from under you with your good foot. If you give it a good shove near the base, it should go down. Okay?"

She swallowed. "Okay. Just tell me when."

The light vanished and she closed her eyes, willing herself to think positively.

"All right—now. Kick it as hard as you can."

Her first attempt was weak, and failed to dislodge the tree, thought it jolted her almost off the ledge. Clinging to her makeshift lifeline, she tried again. This time the tree shifted, bringing fresh pain to her ankle. She bit her lip, brought her knee up as far as she could, and then jammed it hard against the tree trunk. With a horrible scraping sound the tree moved, then with a groan, slid away from her. It seemed an awful long time before she heard the crashing thud of its landing far below.

Her voice had raised several notches when she called out, "It's gone."

"I heard it." Brad sounded grim now. "Can you reach your ski to take it off?"

"I think so." Carefully she bent her right knee and fiddled with the clamps. The shattered ski fell away from her and joined the tree at the bottom of the ravine. "Okay, it's gone, too."

"Then try to stand up. I'll pull as hard as I can. Move real slowly, and try to stay as close to the wall as you can."

She gripped the belt and drew in a deep breath. "I'm ready."

At the first tug of the belt she pulled herself painfully to her feet. Brad's tone was a lot lighter now, and she took heart, even though her stomach seemed to drop at the thought of leaving the fragile security of that ledge.

"You should be able to reach my hands now," Brad said above her.

She looked up, almost into his face. "Hi," she said unsteadily. "And thanks."

"Don't thank me yet," he said gruffly. "I still have to get you out of here."

Once more he lowered his hands toward her. "Take off your gloves. We'll have a better grip."

Quickly she took off the gloves and shoved them in her pockets. Then she reached up and grasped his hands. "I don't have any footholds," she said, striving to sound unafraid. "The wall is as smooth as glass."

"Then I guess brute strength will have to do. Good thing I work out regularly."

For once she was in complete agreement. "I could try jumping," she suggested.

"Too risky. Better let me take your weight and keep as still as you can."

"All right." She swallowed hard as her feet left the ledge and she felt herself hanging from the death grip Brad had on her hands. She heard him grunt as she inched up the wall, then her head cleared the top of the ravine and she could look out at the swirling snow. One more painful jerk on her hands and her upper body was on firm ground. She was safe.

Brad let go of her hands, but before she could drag herself farther out he grabbed her under the armpits and hauled her the rest of the way. They both went down in a heap in the snow where, much against her will, she ended up sprawled on top of him.

For a moment or two it seemed neither of them could get their breath, then Brad said wheezily, "We've got to stop meeting like this."

"Believe me," Anne said, just as breathlessly, "this wasn't planned."

"Aw, and here I thought you were still trying to get my attention." He grinned up at her. "Though I can think of better places to get cozy."

The comment was enough to remind her exactly who he was. She rolled off him and sat up. "I'm very grateful to you for getting me out of there, Brad, but don't think it gives you any special privileges."

She could see his expression quite clearly in the reflection from his headlamp. He actually looked offended, though she couldn't tell if it was genuine or not. "Are you kidding? It was the furthest thing from my mind. I know better than to hit on a Parker. I'm liable to get drawn and quartered.''

"Well, don't let it ruin your evening.'' Miffed in spite of herself, she scrambled unsteadily to her feet.

He got up more slowly. "Can you walk?''

"I think so.'' She hesitated, then added in a rush, "Look, I really am very grateful.''

"No big deal. Just don't tell anyone I rescued a Parker. My mother would never let me forget it.''

She leaned down to massage her ankle. "I'll take care not to mention it to her. But I'm quite sure my family will be very grateful.''

He pulled on his gloves and turned up the collar of his jacket. "I didn't do anything anyone else wouldn't have done, so don't feel you have to take it personally. I wouldn't have left a dog down there to freeze to death.''

Feeling somewhat offended by his cavalier tone, she tested her weight on her ankle. An agonizing shaft of pain made her wince. It was going to be a painful trip back down the mountain. Her voice sharpened. "Well, I'm grateful that you think I was worth saving. I'll share a bone with you when we get back to town. Which can't be soon enough for me.''

"Well, you might have to wait a while for that.'' Light blazed a path across the snow as he turned his head. Thick white snowflakes slanted down the beam, obliterating everything except for a few feet ahead. "We won't get far in this mess tonight.''

She stared at him in alarm. "What are you saying? You're not suggesting we stay the night up here?''

The resignation in his face frightened her. "Looks like it.''

"We can't stay here." She fought a wave of panic. "We'll freeze to death. Besides, everyone will be worried sick. We have to at least try to get back down."

Brad shoved his hands in the pockets of his jacket. "Believe me, there's nothing I'd like better. I should point out, however, that it's snowing like crazy, the avalanche has wiped out the trails, it's dark as blazes and the battery in my headlamp won't last much longer. If that isn't enough, you can't walk on that ankle, and if you think I can carry you down this mountain then I'm afraid you're going to be disappointed. I'm in pretty good shape, but I'm not a superhero. I'm sorry, Your Highness, but like it or not, we're going to be spending the night right here on this mountain."

Chapter 3

Anne had never felt so cold in her entire life. She looked around at the swirling snow, appalled because she knew he was right, yet still unwilling to accept it. "Someone must be looking for us," she said desperately. "If we at least start down they'll spot us sooner or later."

"They won't send anyone out until it's light. It's too dangerous in this snowstorm."

She felt too devastated to answer him. She knew what little chance they had of surviving the night without shelter. Already the freezing wind seeped into her bones, making her movements stiff and awkward.

"Here." Brad pulled a ski cap from his pocket and handed it to her. "I always keep a spare in my pocket. It will help keep your body warmth in."

The gesture took her by surprise, and momentarily

eased the chill inside her. She took it from him with mumbled thanks and pulled it on her head.

"I saw a cabin on my way down here." Brad pointed up the mountain. "It's not too far. Do you think you could make it if I help you?"

Hope flared at once. "I'll make it," she said firmly.

"It doesn't look as if anyone's used the cabin for a long time, but I saw a chimney and we might be able to find a way to light a fire. Can you walk on that ankle?"

Just the thought of being close to a fire made her feel better. She tested her weight on her foot again and gritted her teeth. "I'll manage."

"Here, grab hold of my arm. We need to get out of this snow before we both freeze to death."

Too cold even to answer him, she slipped her gloved hand inside the crook of his arm and stepped gingerly onto her injured ankle. The pain made her nauseous and it took all her self-control not to groan.

Her frown must have betrayed her, however, as Brad clamped his arm around her waist. "Here, lean on me. Try to keep as much weight off your foot as possible."

She had to admit, his presence helped a lot. His hip supported her as they struggled forward in the deep snow, and his grip on her waist propelled her along, while she braced her arm around the small of his back and clung to his soaked jacket.

When he spoke again his deep voice seemed to rumble through her entire body. "I'm sorry, Annie. This has to be tough on a woman like you."

She didn't answer him at first, absorbed in putting one foot in front of the other with as little pain as possible. But after a moment or two, the significance of his comment started to bother her. "What do you mean," she demanded breathlessly, "a woman like me?"

"You know what I mean. All that city living makes people soft. You're obviously not used to the rigors of outdoor activities."

She barely managed to keep her voice even. "And you are, I take it."

"I've had a lot more experience at it than you have, yes."

"Really." She could feel her blood warming up. "Well, it's a little tough to leap buildings with a single bound on a busted ankle."

"Granted. I'm talking about your lifestyle, though."

"And just what do you know about my lifestyle that makes you such an expert on it?"

"Small town. People talk."

"Well, you've been talking to the wrong people." Her foot slipped, almost unbalancing her.

Brad's arm tightened around her waist. "Come on, admit it. You spend your spare time eating out at fancy restaurants or going to the theater. Right? Hardly measures up to climbing a mountain in a snowstorm."

Her lips tightened, or they would have done so if she could have felt them. "I had no idea I led such a boring life. Not at all like yours, of course. Must be very satisfying to be honored as the town's most conspicuous swinging single."

"What's that supposed to mean?"

"It means that some people have a problem growing up."

He grunted something under his breath, and she resisted the urge to ask him what he'd said. She had an idea she'd be better off not knowing.

After a few more yards, he said quietly, "You know, we'll get through this a lot better if we just manage to keep a sense of humor."

Anne rolled her eyes. "My sense of humor would have a better chance of asserting itself if you could keep your mind on practical issues instead of passing judgment on people whom you know nothing about."

"I was just trying to make conversation. It's good for our morale."

"Well, do us both a favor and quit worrying about our morale. We'll both do a lot better without your helpful observations. Besides, I don't have enough breath to talk."

He didn't answer, and again her conscience pricked her. He had, after all, saved her life, and was doing his best to find shelter for her. If she wasn't so darn cold and worried, not to mention in severe pain, she'd handle things better. It didn't help her disposition to be uncomfortably aware of the fact that on some deep, primitive level, the man was having a disturbing effect on her hormones.

The thought of spending the night alone with him in an isolated cabin was actually heating up her blood in spite of the frigid temperature. The very fact that he could arouse those feelings in her when she was so miserably cold and in pain was a testament to his formidable sex appeal. Having listened to her sisters avidly describe some of his conquests in town, however, coupled with the fact that he was an Irving, it shouldn't be too difficult to stay immune to his lethal charm, she assured herself. She'd have to make damn sure to keep remembering his shortcomings. She just hoped and prayed that would be enough.

Brad felt another chill shudder through his body and braced his shoulders against the frigid wind. Snowflakes blew directly into his face and clung to his eyelashes. He shook his head, trying to clear his vision.

In spite of the cheerful front he was trying to keep up, he had no illusions about the urgency of their situation. They were in deep trouble all right. Stranded on a mountain during a whiteout was no picnic at the best of times. Saddled with an injured, helpless female who considered herself far too superior to be on the same mountain as him didn't improve the situation any.

If he'd had any hope at all of getting back to the lodge with her he'd have made the attempt. He'd been around the mountains long enough, however, to know the risks of trying to walk out on foot. Even in good weather and on two good feet it would have been a formidable task.

The trails had probably been covered up by the avalanche, maybe even the lodge as well. It would be too easy to get disoriented and lose all sense of direction. They wouldn't stand a chance out there without food or shelter. As it was, he wasn't at all sure he could find the cabin he'd passed.

All he could do was hope they'd stumble across it

again, and that there were enough supplies to keep them going until they were rescued.

"Is that the cabin up there?" Anne said, pointing to his right. "There's something up there. Or is it just a tree?"

He paused, squinting against the blinding snow. To his enormous relief, he could see the squat, square shape of the cabin against the backdrop of snow. "That's it! Good job. We could have walked right past it without even noticing it."

"I'm glad I'm useful for something."

She'd sounded dispirited and he glanced down at her in concern. She would need all her strength and determination to survive this little jaunt. She wasn't the type to handle these rugged conditions, and he was more than a little worried about how she'd react to the primitive aspects of the next few hours. Especially if those hours stretched into another day.

Though he had to admit, she'd handled her rescue with a lot more fortitude than he would have given her credit for, under the circumstances. If she could hang on to that kind of grit for a while, they might just survive the ordeal.

He felt her stumble and tightened his grip on her waist. Even though the parka added padding to her slim body, he was instantly aware of her lithe figure. He had to be crazy. That was the last thing on earth he needed right now. Or any time, come to that, considering who she was.

He gritted his teeth and concentrated on moving one step at a time toward the cabin, which loomed up slowly in the darkness. Only a few more yards to go. He was practically carrying her now, and he was worried she'd give up altogether before they made it to their broken-down shelter.

"Hang on, it's not much further," he muttered, trying to form the words between harshly drawn breaths. His legs felt as if they were weighted down in lead boots. His back ached and his jaw hurt from clenching his teeth to stop them chattering. He longed for a shot of double-malt scotch, and could almost feel the heat of it coating his stomach. That was only one of the things he'd have to do without, he thought grimly.

At long last, he reached the front steps of the cabin and could release his heavy load. "Well, Annie," he said, forcing an enthusiasm in his voice he was far from feeling, "it looks like we made it."

"Thank God." She was panting, and her words came out in little spurts. "I don't think I could have gone another step."

Brad eyed the cabin with a dubious frown. The windows were cracked and layered with dust, and the roof probably leaked. Its primitive walls, fashioned from logs, looked sturdy enough, however, and would give them shelter until help arrived. He had no doubt that at least for the time being, the most sensible thing to do was to stay put and wait for the rescue squad.

It wouldn't be a picnic, by any means. His companion was as prickly as a porcupine, and made no secret of the fact that she considered him too low to lick her boots. He wasn't sure how long he could hold his temper in the face of such undisguised contempt. He just hoped that he could hang on to his sense of humor, and that they wouldn't kill each other while they were waiting.

Anne sank down onto the creaking wooden step

and buried her face in her hands. She couldn't have gone another step. In fact, if it hadn't been for Brad's arm supporting her, she wouldn't have made it this far.

She owed him a lot. The thought didn't help her mood any. He was bound to be insufferable about it when this was all over.

"How are you doing?"

She looked up at the sound of his voice. "I'll be fine when I've had a chance to rest."

"Well, don't get too comfortable." He rattled the handle of the door. "First we have to find a way inside this shack, then we have to find some way to build a fire."

"Wouldn't that be breaking and entering?" She looked warily at the battered windows. "What if the owner comes back in the morning?"

"We'll welcome him with open arms." He shook his head at her, spraying fine drops of water from the melted snow in his dark blond hair. "This is survival, Annie. The owner will understand that."

"What if he's in there, sleeping?"

"Then he's deaf." Brad moved over to a window and ran his fingers along the edge. "I pounded the heck out of the door on my way down."

She stared at him as a thought occurred to her. "Why didn't you break in then? Why did you keep going instead of waiting out the storm in here?"

He kept his face hidden from her as he examined the window. "I was looking for you."

She felt a jolt of surprise. "You mean you didn't just stumble across me by accident?"

"Well, I have to admit, there was a certain element

of luck to it. I lost sight of everyone when the first wave hit. I got thrown around a bit and when I surfaced I saw your broken ski. I figured you couldn't be too far away.''

She frowned. "How did you know it was my ski? It could have been anyone's. It could have been your girlfriend's. Where is she, by the way?"

"What girlfriend?"

"The giggling redhead making a fool of herself out there with you."

He glanced at her. "Oh, you mean Marlene. She's not my girlfriend. She's just someone I got paired up with for the midnight run."

"How convenient for you."

"I'm surprised you noticed."

Anne pretended to be examining her injured ankle. "She was a little hard to miss, considering the way she was falling all over you."

"Jealous?"

She managed a scornful laugh. "The only thing I'd be jealous about is if she'd made it down the mountain and was lying in a comfortable bed in the lodge."

"Which is probably where she is right now. The last I saw of her she was heading through the trees well out of the way of the avalanche."

"Well, good for her," Anne muttered.

"Which is why I knew the broken ski didn't belong to her. Besides, only a Parker would have custom-made skis in hot pink."

"Only an Irving would make such a big deal about it."

Her comeback was lost as Brad straightened with

a satisfied grunt. The window emitted a loud crack and creaked open.

"You didn't break it, did you?" Hanging on to the wall, Anne hauled herself to her feet.

"Nope, so you can stop worrying about the owner suing us. It wasn't even locked, just frozen shut, which is the way we're going to be if we don't get a fire started soon."

Anne watched as he poked his head inside the window, then heaved himself over the sill and climbed inside. Within seconds he opened the door.

Doing her best to disguise her limp, she stepped over the threshold into the damp, musty darkness of the cabin. The beam from Brad's headlamp had weakened considerably when he directed it around the confined area.

There was enough light for Anne to make out the woodstove in the middle of the room and the rickety-looking cot tucked into the far corner. Apart from that, there appeared to be no other furniture, except for a small square table and a couple of cheap wooden chairs. She couldn't really see thick cobwebs hanging in the corners, but she had no doubt they were there.

"Not exactly Club Med, is it?" Brad murmured.

If her spirits hadn't been at an all-time low, then, Anne might even have smiled at that. Right then, however, she couldn't see much to smile about. The cabin felt almost as damp and cold as the air outside, and smelled of mold and wood smoke.

The narrow cot seemed to be the only bed available, and the only covering was a ratty looking blanket folded at the bottom of the thin mattress. A cell in Alcatraz would have been more comfortable, and as if that wasn't enough, she had to spend what was left of the night there with Brad Irving, of all people. All in all, the year was ending on a pretty dismal note.

"First thing we'd better do is find wood for a fire." Brad flicked the beam of his headlamp over Anne's boots. "How's the ankle?"

Still smarting from his assessment of her dubious athletic abilities, Anne lied. "It's fine."

"Good. I'll get the wood. No sense in both of us going out there again. You can stay there on that cot until I get back."

The last thing she wanted was to be left alone in the cold darkness of that awful cabin. It would, however, give her a chance to rest her ankle. Nevertheless, she felt compelled to offer her help. "It might be easier if we both went."

"I'll manage. I don't want you wandering off and getting lost in the dark." He pointed to his head. "This is the only light we have left."

He made it sound as if she'd lost her own headlamp on purpose. Annoyed, she glared at him, though she could barely see his face. "I wish you would stop treating me as if I were helpless. For your information, I've been camping in the wilderness before, and I grew up skiing on these mountains. I'm not totally clueless about the outdoors."

The irony in his voice was hard to miss when he answered her. "Right. My guess would be that your idea of camping is an air-conditioned trailer, complete with TV, and I'm willing to bet you've spent more time in the lodge than you have on the slopes."

Damn him, he was right. According to her sisters, Brad had spent at least two summers backpacking in the high country and one camping in Alaska during his college years. Until now, the closest she'd come to actually roughing it was a canoe trip on a quiet stretch of the Colorado.

The door creaked open, letting in a blast of cold air. He paused in the doorway, silhouetted against the snow-laden branches of the trees outside. "Just stay put until I get back. That way you won't fall over anything."

Closing the door behind him, he left her frowning in the cold, damp darkness of the cabin. He talked as if she were a prize klutz. As if it were her fault the avalanche had thrown her into a ravine. And if he didn't quit with the patronizing she was going to hit him over the head with his precious headlamp.

She waited awhile, sitting on the edge of the cot until her temper cooled, and she could think straight again. Across the room she could just make out some shelves on the wall, and something faintly gleaming in the light reflected by the snow outside.

Deciding to investigate, she tested her weight on her injured ankle. The pain made her wince, but it wasn't enough to prevent her from limping across the room. As she approached the shelves she caught sight of something hanging on the wall next to them. Her spirits rose considerably when she realized it was an oil lamp, and there were actually matches sitting in the saucer.

She pulled the lamp from the wall, and shook it, half expecting it to be empty. The sound of oil swishing around inside reassured her. The matches were damp, but she finally got one alight and seconds later a soft glow lit up the room.

Just having enough light to see made her feel warmer, even though her teeth refused to stop chattering. She pulled off her hat and tucked it in her pocket, then inspected the items on the shelves. An aluminum bucket sat on one end, next to a cooking pot and a frying pan. The plastic mugs and plates had the patterns worn off them, but were otherwise clean and serviceable. Several spoons stood inside one of the mugs and much to her delight, she discovered a jar of dried soup mix and another full of rice, tucked behind a large, slightly rusted can of cocoa. There were even a half dozen toilet rolls still in the original wrapper. Things were beginning to look a little less bleak.

At least they wouldn't starve. Though with any luck they wouldn't need the food. They'd both eaten dinner before they'd left for the ski run, and the search party would be out at first light. It would just be a matter of time before someone spotted the cabin and came to investigate. All they had to do was keep the fire going, she assured herself, determined to remain optimistic.

Having satisfied herself that she'd checked everything out on the shelves, she returned to the cot, and sat there for several minutes. She was just beginning to get seriously worried about Brad when a sharp rap on the door made her jump. She limped across the room to let him in, and was instantly cheered by the sight of the armful of wood he carried.

"You found matches," he exclaimed, as he stepped inside the room. "I thought I'd have to start a fire with two sticks."

"I'm glad we don't have to rely on that," Anne

murmured, slamming the door against the driving snow. "We'd be waiting all night. Or is that another of your remarkable talents?"

He grunted, and dropped the wood in front of the stove. "You haven't even begun to see my talents yet."

"Thank the Lord for small mercies."

"You might be grateful for my capabilities before this adventure is over."

"Remind me to be suitably impressed."

Snow caked his ski cap, and he pulled it off and shook his head, spraying drops of water around him. "Is that the thanks I get for rescuing you?"

She was instantly ashamed of her pettiness. "Sorry. I know you're doing your best. I'm cold and miserable, and I guess I feel pretty helpless. It's not a feeling I'm comfortable with."

His smile seemed to light up the entire room. "Apology accepted. Ankle hurting you?"

She nodded, feeling an idiotic urge to cry. "A little."

"Okay, let me just get this fire going and I'll take a look at it. I don't suppose you found any paper lying around?"

She had a tough time keeping the gloating out of her voice when she answered him. "As a matter of fact, I did find a couple of newspapers." Her gesture at the shelves sent him heading over there.

"Heck, there's an abundance of goodies here." He poked around for a bit then came back with a newspaper in his hand. "You'll be surprised how much better you'll feel once you're warm again. Wish I had some brandy to offer you. That would really help to warm your insides.''

"There's some cocoa over there.'' She nodded at the shelves. "There's no running water in here, though.''

Brad stacked the smaller pieces of the wood inside the stove and made a pyramid of them. "I imagine there's a stream somewhere nearby. I doubt if anyone would build a cabin without a water supply within reach. I wouldn't want to go looking for it tonight, though. It would be too easy to get lost out there.''

"Perhaps we could melt some snow?''

She felt a silly rush of pleasure at his glance of approval. "Good thinking. I'll get some when we get the fire going.''

"I can get it. I found a bucket over there, among other things.'' She started to limp across the room but he halted her with a sharp command.

"No! I don't want you going anywhere on that ankle tonight. Just sit tight and I'll take care of everything.''

Exhaustion urged her to obey him, and she dropped onto the end of the cot. She watched him in silence as he worked at getting the fire alight.

He seemed unaware of her scrutiny, intent on coaxing the damp, smoldering twigs to burst into flame. He squatted on his heels and leaned forward, puffing his cheeks to blow on the thin wisp of smoke rising from the grate.

His hands were strong and capable, resting on muscled thighs clearly defined beneath the stretched fabric of his black ski pants. His fur-lined jacket stretched across his broad shoulders, the upturned collar almost hiding his face. He seemed in complete control of the situation, almost to the point of enjoying it, though she sensed a thin layer of apprehension beneath the bantering front he'd no doubt adopted for her benefit.

He was the kind of man women adored—amusing, charming, good-looking, attentive and a rock under stress. And from what she'd heard, not in the least bit interested in commitment.

Without warning the memory was back, almost as hurtful as it had been the day it happened. Jason, emerging from her best friend's bedroom with a mixture of guilt and relief on his face. Guilt at being caught, and no doubt relief that now he had an excuse not to go through with the wedding. She would never again risk her heart for that kind of pain.

"Well, aren't you going to applaud?"

She started, realizing that Brad had stood and was watching her with an odd expression on his face. Behind him the yellow glow of tiny flames licked up the stack of wood.

"You did it!" she exclaimed, clasping her hands to her heart in mock admiration. "My hero!"

He pulled a face. "Don't think it was that easy, either. That wood is as wet as a soaked sponge." Despite his grudging tone, he looked immensely pleased with himself.

Anne studied the fragile flames. "I hope it stays alight long enough to warm up this place. It's freezing in here."

"Ah, well, that's the thing. That's all the wood I could find out there. Most of the dead stuff is buried under the snow. The fire's not going to last longer than an hour or so.'' He glanced over at her. "Looks like we'll be sharing that cot tonight to keep warm.''

Anne felt as if all the breath had suddenly squeezed out of her lungs. The cot was no more than three feet wide. There was barely room for one person, let alone two. Well, if he was hoping to turn this into one of his infamous nights of passion he was out of luck. There was no way she was going to spend what was left of the night jammed up tight next to Brad Irving's treacherous and highly seductive body. She'd freeze first.

Chapter 4

"Well," Brad said heartily, as if he were completely unaware he'd said anything controversial, "let's take a look at that ankle."

Still totally off balance, Anne could only stare up at him in growing dismay.

"I only want to look at it." He seemed a little unsure of himself for once as he pulled a clean, white, folded handkerchief from his pants pocket. "I'll bind it up with this. You really need some support for it."

Right then she didn't want him anywhere near her, much less touching her ankle, but there didn't seem to be any way to tell him that without sounding totally paranoid. Telling herself that she would deal with the issue of the cot later, she reluctantly stretched out her injured foot.

"This might hurt," Brad said, as he squatted in front of her. "I'll be as gentle as I can."

"It's okay," Anne said unsteadily. "I'm tougher than I look."

His expression said clearly that he doubted that, but she was too apprehensive to argue the fact. She watched him unbuckle her ski boot, and tried not to wince as he dragged it off her foot. She kept a stoic face as he drew off her sock, but no matter how hard she tried, she couldn't prevent the tremor when his fingers touched the bare skin of her ankle.

"Sorry," he said quickly. "It's a little puffy but I don't think anything's broken. Just a bad sprain, though you won't be walking on it for a while."

"Not without a lot of pain, anyway." Her voice shook, much to her annoyance. She hated to admit that her uneasiness was due more to the gentle, almost caressing touch of his fingers than any pain she was feeling right then.

She looked down on the top of his head as he carefully bound her ankle with his handkerchief. He was close enough for her to detect the faint fragrance of his aftershave. Close enough to notice the way his hair curled behind his ears. Close enough to reach out and touch the smooth line of his jaw.

What on earth was the matter with her? Hadn't she learned the lesson of a lifetime from Jason's betrayal to stay immune to that kind of lethal charm? So what if Brad had a body a wide receiver would envy. So what if his smile could curl her insides. According to the town gossip, Brad Irving was about as sincere as a car salesman and just as much a womanizer as Jason. She'd do well to remember that.

Brad chose that moment to look up, straight into

her eyes. "There," he said softly. "How does that feel?"

Fantastic, her mind sighed. "Better," she said briskly. "Thanks."

"You're welcome." He leaned his hands on his thighs and pushed himself to his feet. "Now I'll get snow to melt, enough to make cocoa, anyway, and we'll have a nightcap before we go to bed."

Anne swallowed hard. "Er…about the cot. It's a little…small, don't you think? Wouldn't it be better if one of us slept on the floor?"

Brad's eyebrows raised a half inch. "The *floor?* On what? Do you have any idea how cold that floor will get once the fire goes out? Not to mention how hard it is."

She eyed him warily. "I thought you were used to roughing it."

"Oh, you're suggesting *I* sleep on the floor. I thought you were offering to take it for yourself."

Frowning, she wondered if he was making fun of her again. "You're the one who's always bleating about how tough you are. How well you adapt to the rigors of outdoor activities."

"Not without a sleeping bag," Brad said grimly. "Forget it, Annie. We share the cot." As if declaring an end to the discussion, he crossed the room to the shelves and took down the bucket.

Feeling mutinous, she studied the floor and wondered which would be the lesser ordeal.

After a moment he added, with just a hint of sarcasm, "Don't worry, I'm not going to molest you, if that's what you're worried about."

Miffed by his perception of her adolescent fears,

she uttered a dry laugh. "You wouldn't live long if you tried."

"That," Brad said heavily, "I can believe. But in this case, it's a moot point. I like my women to be...shall we say...a little more enthusiastic?"

"You mean hot to trot."

He grinned. "And I was under the impression that you were a lady."

To her intense irritation, she actually felt offended that he considered her unworthy of his advances. But then that could be just part of the plan. Lull her into a false sense of security, then pounce when she wasn't expecting it. She bent over and retrieved her sock, then pulled it carefully over the bandaged foot. "I trust you'll remember that," she said lightly.

"Believe me, I'm not about to forget it. If there was any other alternative to sleeping with you, I'd take it. But I'm not about to spend the rest of the night on that floor. I promise you, your reputation will remain intact. After all, who's going to know? If there's one thing I've learned in my profession, it's how to keep my mouth shut. As long as you do the same, you have nothing to worry about."

Just the fact she'd spent the night under the same roof as an Irving, not to mention the town's most prominent playboy, was enough to raise some pretty intense speculation, Anne thought wryly. Especially among the members of her family.

Still unsure whether or not she could trust him, she watched him cross the room to the door.

"I'll get the snow," he said, pausing to glance back at her. "Keep an eye on the fire for me. I'll be back in a minute or two." He pulled the ski cap from his pocket, jammed it on his head and before she could answer him, he'd closed the door with a bang behind him.

Once he was out in the twisting, twirling snow-flakes, Brad pulled in a deep breath of frigid air. He had no idea why, but there was something about that lady in there that could almost make him forget who she was.

He had to be crazy. One wrong move and she'd have the entire Parker family down on his head, screaming assault, or worse. He stomped down the steps, one hand clinging to the railing as his feet sank into inches of new snow. He had no illusions about her opinion of him. None at all.

Reaching the bottom of the steps, he peered across the clearing. In the reflection from the dim light spilling from the dusty windows he could see the branches of the firs almost touching the ground with the weight of the snow.

The avalanche had deposited enough of the wet stuff to almost reach the roof. If it kept snowing at this rate, it would be tough to spot the cabin by morning. He would just have to get out at first light and find enough wood to keep a fire going.

He waded through deep drifts toward the trees, where the snow lay in a smooth, unbroken carpet. Holding the bucket by one edge, he skimmed it along the surface until he'd almost filled it. With one hand he packed it down hard, then scooped up more snow, packing it down until the bucket was filled to the brim. Just for good measure he piled even more on top, then picked up the bucket and tramped back to the cabin.

He wasn't looking forward to the night ahead of him. If he'd been stranded with anyone but Annie Parker, this little adventure might have been bearable. As it was, the next few hours promised to be uncomfortable at best.

The family feud aside, he had the feeling her animosity toward him was highly personal. She had always treated him with barely concealed contempt, ever since grade school, but now it was more than just the fact he was an Irving. She seemed to think he was planning to jump her bones at any second.

Some women might enjoy that, he thought ruefully as he stomped up the steps, but not Annie Parker. She acted as if he might contaminate her if he came too close. She'd made it quite clear that she trusted him about as much as she'd trust a hungry bear.

Granted, he'd been known to date a few women in his time, but that didn't make him a compulsive letch, did it? What was the matter with her? Was she that hung up on her own body image she thought every man was dying to jump into bed with her?

By the time he got the door open again he'd worked up a pretty healthy resentment, and it didn't help much to notice the wariness on Annie's face when he stepped into the room.

He crossed over to the stove and dumped the bucket on the hot plate. "This should be enough to melt down for cocoa," he said, without looking at her. "Though I don't know how long it will take to boil with this puny little fire."

''That's okay. I'm pretty sleepy anyway. I don't think I'll need the cocoa.''

He nodded. ''I guess we can leave it there until morning. The fire won't last much longer, so I'll have to go look for wood as soon as it's light.''

''I'll help. My ankle should feel better by tomorrow.''

''Don't count on it.'' He pulled his cap from his head. ''Those sprains can be painful for days.'' Now that it was time to actually get into bed, he was suddenly wide-awake. He gathered up the wood that was left and shoved it all inside the stove. ''That will have to do for now.'' He made himself turn around and look at her.

She sat on the cot with her back to the wall. She'd taken off her other boot, and had pulled her knees up under her chin with her arms wrapped around them. The zipper of her blue ski jacket was undone, revealing a plum-colored sweater underneath.

She leaned forward, letting her sun-streaked hair fall across her shoulders. The silky mass framed her face, and her beautiful green eyes looked at him anxiously as he moved toward her. He felt a tug deep in his belly, and cursed his animal instincts. Annie Parker was way off-limits…and it was just as well.

Right then she looked soft and vulnerable, and infinitely inviting. His hands itched to stroke that soft hair, slide the heavy jacket from her shoulders, follow the enticing contours of her body…. He stopped short, appalled by the sensual journey his mind was taking. That kind of thinking was dangerous, and could lead to all kinds of trouble.

As if reading his thoughts, she said nervously, "It will probably be warmer to sleep in our jackets."

"Probably, but not very comfortable." He unzipped his jacket, slid it off his shoulders and let it drop to the floor. "You do whatever you want, though."

She straightened her back, pressing it against the wall. "I'll keep mine on for now," she said faintly.

"Suit yourself." He took the last, fateful step toward the cot and sat down to take off his boots. He could almost feel her tension when he eased himself carefully down on the very edge of the bed. Even so, his shoulder came in hard contact with her legs. She immediately shifted them away from him and he frowned. This was going to be one hell of a long night.

"What do you think happened to the lodge?" she mumbled, in a voice that sounded as if she had been swallowing dust. "Do you think the avalanche did any damage?"

He wasn't sure how to answer that question. The lodge had been in the direct path of the tumbling snow. The chances of it escaping the onslaught altogether were pretty slim. Shifting onto his back, he raised his hands and tucked them behind his head. "It's hard to say, but the lodge is solidly built and has survived a lot of winters up here. I'd figure on it holding up. The avalanche would have slowed down considerably by the time it reached the lower slopes."

"I hope everyone made it down," Anne said soberly.

He glanced up at her. She'd buried her chin in her knees again, and he couldn't read her expression, but he knew by her voice she was worried about her family. "I'm about as certain as I can be that you were the only one caught by the snow. I was the last one to take off, and I saw everyone veering off for the trees at the first crack. You were the only one to keep going until it was too late."

She sighed. "Stupid, I know. But I just couldn't believe it was happening. It was so dark, I didn't see it coming until it was too late."

"Well, that's where experience comes in. The sound alone warned the rest of us."

"How long do you think it will be before they find us?"

He shrugged. "With any luck, early tomorrow morning. It depends on how much snow we get tonight."

"What if they don't find us?"

"They'll find us," he said, with a lot more conviction than he felt.

"But what if they don't?"

"We'll cross that bridge when we come to it." He glanced up at her again but her face was still hidden.

"Worrying about it isn't going to help, Annie. Try to get some sleep. Things will look a hell of a lot better once it's daylight. I promise you."

"I hope so."

"Trust me." Wrong thing to say, he thought wryly, as she lifted her chin and gave him a sardonic glance. "I'm going to turn the lamp out." He leaned over the side of the bed to reach it. "No sense in wasting the oil." He didn't mention that they might need the lamp again if their rescue was delayed. There was no point in adding to her worry. He turned the wick down and the flame flickered and died, leaving only the faint glow from the stove to light the room.

Anne sat where she was for another minute or two, reluctant to give up the security of the wall at her back. She was being childish, she knew, but she couldn't seem to help it. The thought of snuggling down for the night next to Brad's formidable body gave her goose bumps.

Her thick quilted jacket was becoming uncomfortably hot, now that the room had warmed up, but she couldn't bring herself to take it off. The more clothes she had between her and Brad the better.

Weariness forced her eyes closed and she felt her head nod forward. She jerked awake, and glanced at the man by her side. He hadn't moved in the last few minutes. While she was still trying to figure out if he was asleep, she heard him gently snore.

Moving an inch at a time, she slid out of her jacket, then eased herself down the bed until she was lying full length with her back to him. It was impossible to lie there without coming in contact with him, and her skin tingled everywhere their bodies touched.

If she hadn't been so exhausted, she would have balanced herself on the extreme edge of the cot, but before she could even think that through, she was asleep.

Brad heard her deep, even breathing, and quit the snoring. He'd pretended to be asleep because he knew she wouldn't relax until she thought he was unconscious. That's how much she trusted him, he told himself ruefully. Whoever had filled her in on the town gossip had done a real hatchet job.

Probably those sisters of hers. Whenever they crossed his path they stared at him as if he were carrying a sign that read, "Beware! Pervert!"

Of course, her entire family would be quick to give her the worst possible picture of him. Damn that stupid feud. It was time both families put an end to it. It served no purpose and had caused everyone nothing but anger and pain for the best part of the last century.

Take the woman lying so peacefully next to him. If it hadn't been for the feud, they might have grown up friends instead of sworn enemies. At least, she might not have been so eager to believe the worst of him.

Right then he couldn't seem to think about anything except her haunting fragrance. It reminded him of the warm night air after the soft caress of summer rain.

He was painfully aware of every seductive curve that came in contact with him. There was a lot to be said for shared body heat. Especially if that body was a warm, appealing woman with eyes that promised far more than their owner would admit.

Brad stifled a groan as his imagination took wing. Somehow he had the idea that Annie Parker was capable of some pretty heated passion. Hungry and aroused, she'd be an exciting prospect. Just thinking about it heated his blood. His lower body stirred, warning him he was probably in for a sleepless night. He closed his eyes and tried to think about something less disturbing than Annie's naked thighs wrapped around his hips.

Anne woke up with a start, instantly aware that something was different, but not certain what it was.

Then she realized her cheek was snuggled against a man's warm back, while her arm rested across his hard, flat stomach. Memory returned in a rush, and her cheeks burned when she realized her knees were tucked firmly under Brad's, in a highly intimate way.

Above the threadbare blanket that covered them her shoulders were cold, but the rest of her burned with an intense, throbbing heat. She was afraid to move, in case she woke him up. She couldn't hear him breathing and prayed he was asleep.

The room was dark, the fire apparently having gone out some time ago. A faint glow outside the smeared windows told her it was getting light, and she longed to know what time it was. There was no point in trying to look at her watch, even if she risked moving her arm, since she wouldn't be able to read the face.

She was hungry, she realized. The thought of fried bacon and eggs, crispy hash browns and hot coffee made her mouth water. With any luck the rescuers would be there early enough for them to get breakfast at the lodge. If there was a lodge still standing.

Then again, there was no point in worrying about something that might not have happened. She'd just have to wait for the rescue squad to get there to find out what had happened to her family. In the meantime, she had a dire need to use the bathroom.

Except there was no bathroom in the cabin. Which meant she'd have to go outside in the snow. The thought of going out in that cold, damp air kept her where she was for a few minutes longer, while she tried not to notice how Brad's body expanded and contracted with every breath.

She couldn't let him wake up and find her plastered against him like this. Somehow she had to get out of the bed without disturbing him. Very carefully, and holding her breath, she withdrew her arm, then eased herself away from him, sliding backward off the cot.

He hadn't moved, and she let out her breath on a quiet sigh of relief. The room was freezing, she could see her breath forming in front of her in a cloud of steam. The light filtering through the dust modes was stronger now, and she could see the interior of the cabin quite clearly. She'd been right about the cobwebs.

Shuddering, she reached for her jacket, which had provided a makeshift pillow for her head. Part of it was tucked under Brad's head, too, and she hesitated before tugging at it.

"Don't go too far from the cabin."

His deep voice made her jump, and with a rush of confusion she realized he'd been awake all along. "I won't," she said unsteadily. "I just have to take care of some personal matters."

He rolled onto his back and looked at her through gold-tinged eyelashes. "I'll wait for you to get back. How's the ankle?"

"Better." For the first time she tested her weight and winced. "Better than it was last night, anyway."

"I'd stay off it as much as possible. When you get back I'll see if I can find some wood for the fire."

"I won't be long." She dragged her jacket on, wondering what on earth she must look like with her hair all tangled up and all traces of makeup washed off by the driving snow. Limping heavily, she headed

for the shelves, pocketed a toilet roll, then crossed to
the door and tugged it open.

Snowflakes danced all around her, and she saw
with dismay that several inches had fallen since last
night. The steps were almost hidden by the drifts,
which had piled up high against the walls of the
cabin. "It's really deep out here." She peered up at
the leaden sky. "The rescue squad will have a hard
time finding us."

"Will you be okay on that ankle? Or do you need
me to come with you?"

She sent him a suspicious glance. He was sitting
up, knees bent, a look of pure innocence on his face.
His black, crewneck sweater was rumpled and his hair
needed a comb. With his heavy-lidded eyes and shad-
owed jaw, he looked every inch the heartbreaker her
sisters had described so avidly.

And that's exactly what he was, she reminded herself fiercely. "I'll manage, thanks."

"Give me a yell if you get stuck out there."

"Sure." Not unless it was a matter of life and
death, she added silently. She stepped out into the
cold, damp air and dragged the door shut behind her.

It took her several minutes to find an appropriate
place behind a thick clump of trees. The mountain
was eerily quiet, with not even the chirp of a bird to
break the silence. It was as if she were completely
alone in this strange, white world, with only that tiny
cabin for refuge against the daunting power of the
mountain.

She'd heard stories of climbers and skiers lost on
these desolate slopes, never to be seen again. Those
who were found rarely survived the ordeal without

serious injury. Brad had been lucky to find the cabin. She had been extremely fortunate that he'd come looking for her, for she surely would have died in that ravine. She owed him her life.

Grabbing handfuls of snow, she scrubbed her face and hands. Her skin stung with the icy dousing, but she felt a little less grungy for her efforts.

How could she repay someone who'd saved her life, she wondered, as she struggled back to the wind-swept shack, which was now half-buried in the snow. Especially someone who might misinterpret her grat-itude for something else. Brad Irving was conceited enough to think that she was as much under the spell of his overrated magnetism as the rest of his entou-rage of women. Any softening in her attitude toward him was bound to be taken the wrong way.

Maybe now, though, since he had rescued her from the jaws of the mountain, her family could forget their differences with the Irvings, and consider the debt paid in full. Surely, Dan Parker would concede that his daughter's life was well worth his pride and call off the silly feud.

If so, then all this discomfort and fear would have been worthwhile. Though it would take both families to truly settle things. Somehow she couldn't see Dar-lene Irving being gracious about anything.

She would have to find a way to repay Brad, she thought soberly, without giving him the idea she was interested in him personally. He *had* been awfully sweet to her, binding up her foot and showing concern for her well-being. This was a side of Brad she hadn't expected to see.

Reaching the steps, she gazed unseeing at the deep

hollows of her own footprints. She was beginning to warm up her opinion of him. That was dangerous. True, he'd spent the entire night by her side without making a move on her. But no matter how sweet and attentive he was, she had to hold on to her convictions.

He could just be playing a waiting game. With men like Brad, everything was a game, with only one objective. And once he'd satisfied his curiosity, established his territory, he'd cast aside his conquest and look for new prey to feed his male ego. To men like Brad, commitment was a season ticket to Mile High Stadium.

Unlike Jason, he might not go as far as to propose marriage in order to get what he wanted, but there wasn't a doubt in her mind where Brad's intentions were headed. Well, this was one woman who wasn't going to fall for that phoney *let-me-take-care-of-you-for-the-rest-of-your-life* act. She'd done that once. And once was more than enough.

A gust of chilly wind broadsided her back, and she hurried up the steps, anxious to be back in the shelter of the cabin. She stumbled on her injured ankle as she pushed open the door and fell into the room. She might have sprawled on the floor if it hadn't been for Brad, who must have been watching for her to return. He caught her under the arms and set her back on her feet.

"Whoa," he said huskily, "what's your hurry?"

For a tense moment she stood frozen to the spot. He was still holding her, his wrists barely brushing the curve of her breasts. She saw something almost feral flash in his eyes, and stopped breathing. For a wild moment she wondered if he would try to kiss her, and if he did, if she would have the strength to resist.

Rattled by her potent reaction to him, she raised her hands and gave him a gentle shove in the chest. "I'm okay. Now it's your turn to brave the elements. It's hard going out there, and it's pretty cold. The temperature must have dropped again."

He let her go at once, his expression once more bland. "I've made the bed," he said, gesturing at the cot. "Thought I'd leave the cleaning up for you."

"How terribly thoughtful of you." She watched him shrug on his jacket and pull up the zipper. "By the way, there's an axe out there on the porch. It's kind of buried, but it looks as if it might be okay."

"I saw it last night." He stepped out onto the landing. "It might take me a while to find some wood, so don't worry if I'm not back right away."

For some ridiculous reason, she felt she was being abandoned. As long as he'd been within shouting distance she'd felt relatively secure. She stared anxiously at him, trying to find reassurance in the strong set of his shoulders beneath the turned up collar of his jacket. "You'll be careful?"

Amusement and something she couldn't define gleamed in his eyes. "Aw, and here I thought you couldn't care less about me."

The flip answer restored her composure. "Actually I'm more concerned about the wood you're bringing back. This place is miserably cold."

He sighed. "Just like a woman. Trust her to put her own comfort first. Never mind the poor shmuck who has to go out in the dark, dangerous world to hunt for firewood.''

"Ah, but with your incredible experience and masterful skills this should be a piece of cake.''

"Yeah, right.''

She watched him until he disappeared from sight beyond the trees, a curious ache in her heart she didn't want to define. It would be far too dangerous to analyze any feelings she might have for Brad Irving.

Chapter 5

Anne had cleaned out all of the cobwebs by the time Brad returned. Somehow he'd managed to drag two hefty fir branches back with him. It had felt like hours since he'd trudged off in the blinding snow, but a glance at her watch confirmed that he'd actually been gone about forty minutes.

Even so, she was relieved to see him. The loneliness of that isolated cabin, hemmed in by the snow, had made her feel claustrophobic. She curbed the urge to rush out and greet him as he approached. Instead, she busied herself sorting out the meager food supplies, while she listened to the steady thwack of the axe biting into wood.

When he finally banged on the door, she hurried as best she could across the room to open it, already anticipating the comforting warmth from a fire.

"Now I know why I became a lawyer." He

stepped inside, grunting with the weight of the logs in his arms.

"So you can play God and get paid for it?"

He scowled at her, stamping his feet to dislodge the snow clinging to his boots. "Tell me something, Annie. Do you hate me because I'm an Irving, or because I'm a lawyer?"

Her cheeks felt warm. She didn't know why she was being so antagonistic toward him, except that it seemed her best defense. All the time they were fighting she couldn't be misled by his seduction routine.

"I don't hate you, Brad," she said carefully. "I don't have any specific feelings for you at all, other than a certain gratitude for saving my life."

"Well, don't let that influence you." He crossed the room and dropped the logs down in front of the stove. "I think I'd rather have you hate me than be totally immune to me. Makes life more interesting, don't you think?"

She couldn't read his expression, since he was squatted down with his back toward her, but she had the distinct impression he was making fun of her again. "I just don't want you to get the wrong impression," she said, a little unnerved by her own honesty.

"Oh, I get it." He glanced at her over his shoulder. "You think if you're nice to me I might throw you down on the bed and have my way with you."

Heat rushed up her body at the thought. "The idea never even occurred to me." Her voice was a little too sharp with the lie. "This might come as a shock to you, Brad, but not every woman you meet is panting to make love with you."

"Aw, gee, and here I was under the impression I was irresistible."

"Sorry to disappoint you."

He chuckled—a low, provocative sound that seemed to echo all the way down her spine. "You haven't disappointed me, Annie...yet."

It was definitely time to change the subject. "I don't suppose you saw any signs of the rescue squad?" she asked hopefully.

"Nope. I guess they'll send a chopper out to check the area, as soon as the storm's over. Might take an hour or two, though. It's still snowing pretty hard out there."

"I know." She tried hard to keep her voice as casual as his had been. "It should give up fairly soon, though, don't you think?"

He shrugged, and went on stacking the wood without looking at her. "Hard to say."

Sometimes the storms could last for days. She was grateful to him for not reminding her of that. She limped to the window and stared out at the leaden sky. How terrible it would be to be trapped in this dismal place for days. "Our families must be worried out of their minds," she said soberly.

"I guess so. There's not a whole lot we can do about it, though."

Hearing the match strike, she turned to watch the flames eating up the crumpled newspaper. "If only we had a cell phone, we could have called them."

"I doubt if one would have picked up a signal from here." He leaned forward to blow on the fragile flame.

"Oh, right, I forgot that." She limped over to the

cot and sat down. She felt restless, awkward, ill at ease. If only the darn rescue team would show up and put an end to this ordeal.

"Surely they'll try to find us today."

"I guess, if they can get out." He stood up and shifted the bucket to the center of the hot plate. "This water should heat up fairly fast. Too bad there isn't any coffee."

"Cocoa will have to do, I guess. How do you feel about soup for breakfast?"

"Better than nothing. Unless you want me to go out and snare a rabbit?"

She stared at him, impressed in spite of herself. "You can do that?"

"No."

"Oh." Realizing he'd been kidding, she sighed. "Then I guess the soup will have to do."

"I do have some good news."

She eyed him warily, not certain if he was serious. "Like what?"

"Like I found the stream. It's just a few yards behind the cabin."

"Wonderful!" This time she meant it. "Does that mean we'll have enough water for a proper wash down?"

"Anything your little heart desires, princess." He waved his hand in an exaggerated flourish. "There's also an outhouse of sorts. Not exactly four-star hotel material, but it's a little less primitive than a bunch of trees and you'll at least have some privacy."

"Thank you." She smiled at him. "That actually sounds pretty great."

His gaze lingered on her face long enough to make

her nervous. "You know, you should smile more often," he said at last.

She turned away, before he could see her sudden rush of pleasure. "I'll bear that in mind."

A lengthy pause followed, broken at last by Brad clearing his throat. "Well, I guess I'll go get some more water. Then we can scrub down."

He grabbed one of the cooking pots and strode to the door. "Keep an eye on the fire. We're a little short on matches."

As the door closed behind him, she let out her breath in a rush. Why did everything he said have to sound like an innuendo? That comment about scrubbing down was loaded with implications. Or did he really think they were going to strip in front of each other to get washed? If so, he was going to be badly disappointed.

By the time he came back, the water was hot enough to make cocoa. Anne added the dried soup to the remainder of steaming water and left the pot to boil.

Brad pulled a face when he tasted the cocoa, but drank it down without making one of his usual wry comments. Seated across the table from him, with nothing else to do but wait, Anne cast around for a safe topic of conversation.

Clasping her hands around the mug for warmth, she asked, "What made you decide to be a lawyer?"

He seemed surprised by the question, but after a moment or two he said slowly, "I guess I liked the idea of helping the underdog win."

"I thought you were a corporate lawyer."

"I am. There are underdogs in corporations, too."

"I always thought you'd work for your father."

His silence unnerved her. Aware that she'd touched on a sensitive subject, she tried to think of a different one, but then he said quietly, "So did he. He wasn't too happy when I told him I wanted to go into law. He couldn't see that he was chained to Coldwater, to the extent of neglecting everything else, including his wife and son."

Not knowing what else to say, she murmured, "That must have been hard. I'm sorry."

"So am I. His glance flicked over her. "I promised myself I'd never get that involved with anything that would control my life like that. I saw my father give his life to that business, literally. He never lived to reap any of the rewards. I'm not going to let that happen to me."

"Owning a business doesn't have to be a jail sentence. I guess it depends on how willing you are to compromise."

"It takes more than one person to compromise. It doesn't work if it's all one-sided."

Aware that she was treading on dangerous ground, she still felt compelled to ask, "What about relationships? Do you try to compromise there, too?"

A gleam appeared in his eyes. "I like variety in my relationships. Does that make me such a bad person?"

"I don't know. Does it?"

He shrugged. "From what I've seen of marriage, no matter how much two people love each other, there's eventually a point when it becomes boring, or confining, or both. I saw it in my own parents. My father struggled to make enough money to keep my mother happy. My mother spent money lavishly because her husband was too busy working to pay attention to her. A vicious circle. Neither one of them was happy, yet they were helpless to break the pattern. Becoming trapped in a situation like that is not my idea of a good life.''

''It doesn't have to be that way. My parents have been together for thirty years, and they are perfectly happy together.''

He gave her a cynical look. ''Do you know that, or is that just what they want you to think?''

''I think I'd know if they weren't happy.''

As if tiring of the subject, he said abruptly, ''What about you? Why an architect?''

Unsettled by the sudden change of subject, it took her a while to come up with an honest answer. ''Buildings have always fascinated me. They are a visual statement of the designer, and I like to think that something I've designed will be around long after I'm gone. Kind of like leaving my mark on the world, I guess.'' She smiled. ''Besides, I'm good at it.''

His gaze was intent on her face. ''Any big plans for Grand Springs?''

She shrugged. ''Maybe. I have to find an office first. Preferably one that I can afford.''

''Then you *are* planning on staying on after the holidays?''

''There's nothing for me in Denver anymore.'' She took a sip of her cocoa, avoiding his gaze.

''There's your work. I heard you were making quite a name for yourself there.''

Surprised again by how much he knew about her,

she said diffidently, "Nothing I couldn't do again in Grand Springs."

"Why did you let him run you out of town?"

Startled and on the defensive, she met his gaze. "Jason didn't run me out of town. I chose to go."

"Because you didn't want to be anywhere where he was."

"Something like that." She stared down at her empty mug. "I don't want to talk about it."

"Isn't that letting him control your life? After all, your work was there, your home, your friends—"

Angry now, she lifted her chin. "I said I don't want to talk about it."

He raised his hands. "Sorry. I was just trying to make a point."

"I know what point you were trying to make. That relationships can be just as confining as businesses. But that's only if you let them. Everyone is ultimately in control of their own life."

"Like you were yours?"

"Like I am now." She stared at him defiantly. "Which, I suspect, is more than I can say for you."

His smile flickered across his face. "I think I have it pretty good right now. A career I value, in a town I love, with plenty of friends with whom I can enjoy it all. What more could a man ask?"

"Security. A sense of belonging. Stability."

He shook his head. "That's a woman's view of a good life. Not a man's."

"Speak for yourself."

"Okay." He lifted his mug and drained it. "I guess I am speaking for myself."

Her resentment unsettled her. It was nothing to her

how Brad Irving chose to live his life. He could make Coverboy of the Year for all she cared. "I'll get the soup," she said shortly, and limped over to the stove to check out the pot.

To her relief he kept the conversation on a mundane level throughout their meal. He'd refilled the pots for her, and set them on the stove to heat for their strip wash later. The prospect of that ordeal hovered on her mind, making her responses to his comments vague at best.

She was thankful when they were finished and she had an excuse to leave the table. "I'll take these outside and rinse them off in the snow," she said, picking up the plates. "I can wash them in hot water later."

Brad watched her take the plates over to the door and disappear outside. He'd been pleasantly surprised by the meal she'd served to him. Steaming hot, the beef-and-vegetable soup had been thickened with rice, and tasted much better than he'd anticipated. Even the cocoa hadn't been too awful. It had been years since he'd drank the stuff, but it wasn't nearly as gruesome as he remembered.

All in all, Annie had come through the ordeal so far with a lot more spunk than he'd given her credit for, much to his surprise. In fact, the longer he was around her, the tougher it was to remember where the boundaries lay.

Annie Parker had always been an attractive woman. He'd long been aware of that on an entirely subconscious level, but the warfare between the families, not to mention the fact that she considered him dirt beneath her feet, had successfully buried any stray thoughts he might have had about her. Until now.

Brad propped his chin and studied the object of his appreciation as she came back through the door. Dressed in the rumpled pants and close-fitting sweater, she appeared far more approachable than she had last night at the lodge. There was a softer air about her now, and with her tousled hair and scrubbed clean face, she looked infinitely desirable.

He shifted in his chair as his body responded to his reflections. Being alone with a woman, without any outside source of distraction, could foster all kinds of stray thoughts. No one could really blame him for that. Any healthy, vigorous, hot-blooded male would feel the same way. He was a flesh-and-blood man after all, and Annie was unmistakably a seductive woman.

It bothered him that she had such a low opinion of him, though. He wanted her to know that he wasn't as bad as everyone painted him. The rumors of his promiscuity had been largely fostered by disapproving old biddies who considered any man still unmarried at his age a threat. And perhaps one or two disgruntled women who'd failed to attract his attention, despite their best efforts to trap him.

As far as he was concerned, he led a perfectly normal social life, or as close as one could have in a small town. At least he wasn't like that jerk who'd used her then dumped her at the first opportunity. Unlike that moron, he'd always been honest with his women friends. He'd made sure they understood upfront that he wasn't interested in anything permanent. It was up to them if they wanted to take it further, and on the rare occasion that one did, he figured she was mature enough to deal with it when he bowed out of a relationship. And usually she was.

But Annie had been really hurt by that jerk, he could tell. Any man who could propose marriage, then cheat on his fiancée before they'd even got to the church, deserved to be horsewhipped. No wonder Annie was so defensive.

Apart from the fact he found her physically appealing, he liked her. A lot. Much more than he would have thought possible. She was smart, spunky and not at all the spoiled brat he'd imagined her to be. He really enjoyed sparring with her. She presented an interesting challenge and he'd always enjoyed a good contest.

Being a normal, sensitive kind of guy, he wanted her to like him. He wanted her to forget everything she'd heard about him, forget that he was an Irving, and learn to like him for himself. Without ex-fiancés, or gossip or feuding families getting in the way.

What he needed, he decided, was to gain her trust. Obviously her faith in men had been shaken by her recent bad experience, and he could well understand that.

"We're running low on wood," Annie announced, breaking into his thoughts. "I've put the last logs in the stove."

"I'll go chop some more." He rose to his feet, welcoming the opportunity to do something other than just sit there and wait. "I might have to chop down a couple of small trees if we're here much longer."

"It looks like it's stopped snowing." She limped

over to the window and rubbed the glass pane with her fingers until a clear ragged circle appeared. "I can actually see blue sky out there."

He joined her at the window, and peered through the circle from over her shoulder. "Well, what do you know. They might get out to us today, after all."

"Do you think so?" Her voice raised in excitement, she turned her head, bringing her face so close to his their noses almost touched.

He stayed where he was, perfectly still, hardly daring to breathe. He saw her eyes widen, first in apprehension, then in something else that speeded up his pulse. She couldn't move away from the window without pushing him out of the way, and he wasn't about to move. Not with her looking at him like that. He dropped his gaze to her mouth, and his heart started beating too fast.

An inch or two closer and he could taste those lips, urge them open and find her tongue. He was actually lowering his mouth to hers when he heard the growl of an engine. He paused, unable to believe the lousy timing. She stared up at him, her eyes questioning.

"I think that's a helicopter," he murmured huskily.

"I think it is, too."

Her voice had sounded tight, as if she was having the same trouble breathing as he was. Intrigued by the thought he said softly, "I'd better get out there and signal it."

She nodded, as if in a trance.

The dull roar of the blades resounded in his ears, but he couldn't seem to tear himself away from her. Then something snapped in his mind. Already the sound was fading. "Damn!" He spun around and leapt to the door.

"Hurry," Annie said, a note of desperation in her voice. "He'll be gone in a minute."

He tugged and fumbled with the rusted handle until finally the door flew open. Stumbling down the steps, he shouted and waved his arms, only to see the tail of the helicopter disappear over the rim of the mountain.

"I don't believe it." He looked up the steps to where Annie clung to the railing, staring in dismay at the empty sky. "Sorry, guess I wasn't quick enough."

She lowered her chin as he trudged back up the steps toward her. He could see the frustration in her face and felt a twinge of guilt. "He'll be back," he said, trying to muster a note of conviction. "We'll just keep watch for him. We'll be ready for him next time."

"We wouldn't have missed him this time if we'd been paying attention." She turned her back on him and went back into the cabin.

The cold air seemed to settle in a knot in his stomach. She was angry with him. Damn, he was angry with himself. For one thing, he'd almost done what he'd promised himself he wouldn't do. He'd almost made a move on her. Stupid. And because of that, he'd missed the damn rescue squad. Though he was quite sure that eventually they would be found, it was obviously going to be later now.

He'd lost whatever ground he'd made. Now he had to make it up to her. Without bothering to go back for his jacket, he began dragging some of the wood he'd gathered out into the open.

Inside the cabin, Anne paced up and down, trying to cool her temper. She was more angry with herself than with him, she thought fiercely. If the helicopter hadn't appeared just about then, she might well have done something stupid, like kiss Brad Irving.

As it was, they'd lost a chance to signal to the rescue team, and it could be the next day before they had another chance. Even longer if the snow started again. Damn Brad and his overactive libido. And damn herself for being susceptible to it.

It seemed as if she were struggling through marshy ground, expecting any minute to plunge into the depths of the murky waters. Every time he got too close to her, every time she saw that look in his eyes, she expected him to kiss her. No, she *longed* for him to kiss her.

He confused her, irritated her, frustrated her and made her feel ridiculously inept, yet somehow she just couldn't seem to shake this crazy adolescent churning inside her whenever he came close.

Falling for that treacherous charm would be a huge mistake. She would not end up as one of his infamous conquests. That's all there was to it. This was one lady who wasn't going to be slammed off her feet by a disreputable charmer without an ounce of loyalty in his entire body.

Other women might find him fascinating and irresistible, but she wasn't in the least bit enthusiastic about going to bed with Brad Irving. From now on, she'd keep a clear line between them, and heaven help him if he tried to step over it again.

Her temper had cooled somewhat by the time he came back inside. ''Guess what I did,'' he announced, looking enormously pleased with himself. "Come and see."

He grabbed her arm and dragged her to the door, apparently forgetting in his excitement about her injured ankle. "There, look there. What do you think?"

At first she couldn't see what he was pointing at, then she realized he'd laid out the branches in some kind of signal, though she couldn't read what it said. Nor was she going to wade through those deep drifts to find out.

Brad was acting so pleased with himself, some mean little devil inside her prompted her to deflate his bubble a little. "Gee," she said dryly, "the way you were acting I thought you'd at least built a sled to take us down the mountain."

His eyes narrowed slightly as he closed the door. "Is that so? Well, I'm sorry my feeble efforts don't meet with your approval. Naturally, being a Parker, you expected something much more dramatic. Like the coach and horses your father hired for your graduation, for instance. Now if *that* wasn't pretentious. Trust a Parker to go overboard and make a ridiculous spectacle of himself."

Anne folded her arms and glared at him. "If anyone should know all about making a spectacle of herself it's your mother. I still remember the Holiday Ball when she hung twinkling lights all over herself and went around calling herself the Spirit of Christmas."

Brad sighed. "I have to admit, that was not one of her better ideas. My mother, however, is only an Irving through marriage. None of the true Irvings would make a mistake like that."

"No?" Anne smiled sweetly. "What about your great-aunt Mathilda Irving? Wasn't she the one who had an affair with Al Capone, and rode up and down Fifth Ave in New York on the back of a beer cart waving a banner that said, 'I'm Big Al's Babe'?"

"That was my great-aunt's mother, it was Chicago, it was a milk cart and it's all hearsay, anyway."

"That's not what your father told my grandfather."

"My father was eight years old when he told your grandfather that story. What did he know?"

"Apparently more than you do."

Brad smiled. "Did anyone ever tell you that your eyes sparkle when you're mad?"

Anne snorted. "That's a typical male remark."

"I'm a typical male."

Annoyed because she had no answer to that, she grabbed up her jacket from the cot. "I'm going for a walk. I need some fresh air."

"I'll come with you. You might need some help on that ankle."

"I can manage just fine on my own. With any luck I'll see the helicopter, and this time I'll make sure he sees me. If I have to spend much more time in this crummy cabin I'll need psychological help when I get back to town."

She left the cabin, and plowed into the snowdrifts with grim determination. She would not let him get to her again. She would just ignore him, and pray the helicopter came back for them before she strangled him.

Out of sheer curiosity, she trudged over to the signal Brad had laid out. When she saw it, she pursed her lips. In huge letters he'd spelled out, alongside an arrow pointing to the cabin, Parker's Playhouse.

Chapter 6

After wading through the snow for half an hour, Anne decided she'd had more than enough of the cold wind, and headed back to the cabin. She'd seen no sign of the helicopter, or of anyone else for that matter. Worse, the clouds had descended once more over the mountain and snow had started to fall again.

It would be dark again soon, and all hope of being rescued that day would be gone. It looked very much as if she would have to spend another night in the cabin with that idiot.

With a jolt she remembered that tonight would be New Year's Eve. The night she was supposed to have celebrated with her family. The night that was supposed to herald in a whole new chapter in her life.

Instead of that, she thought morosely, she was facing another night in the wilderness with an immature comedian who couldn't seem to take anything seriously. She didn't know what bothered her more, the fact that he seemed so unconcerned, or that his cavalier attitude actually mattered to her. Either way, she thought uneasily, she was in big trouble.

Reaching the cabin, she stole quietly up the steps. If he'd decided to take a nap, she didn't want to disturb him. Moving carefully, she pried open the door and peered in. What she saw wiped out all coherent thought from her mind.

Brad stood by the stove with his back to her—wearing absolutely nothing. Fortunately he was in the process of sluicing himself down with water from the pot and didn't seem to notice his silent witness.

Frozen to the spot, she hesitated for several head-spinning seconds, taking in the long, lean line of his back and strong, muscled shoulders, rippling with every move. His fading tan, she noticed, reached almost to the curve of his firm buttocks, where the lighter skin stretched taut across his hips.

The loud snap of a log in the stove jolted her out of her trance. Feeling as if she were about to suffocate, Anne slowly backed out, praying he hadn't heard her. Just before she could shut the door, his teasing voice jarred her frazzled nerves.

"Where are you going, Annie? I need you to scrub my back."

Closing her eyes, she pulled the door shut and leaned against it. He'd known she was there all the time. No doubt enjoying her discomfort. Damn him. No matter what else she tried to concentrate on, nothing could erase the vision in her mind of his well-proportioned body and its graceful curves.

This had to stop. She couldn't take much more of

this. He seemed to be drawing her into his game of seduction, without even trying. Unless he'd had it all planned out. After all, it would have been simple enough to wait until he saw her approach the cabin and stage that whole thing. Damn him again. He was just too good at this.

She waited for what seemed like hours on that cold, damp landing, watching the snow drift down through the thick branches of the firs. Nerves tight, she jumped violently when the door suddenly opened.

"What are you doing out there?" Brad demanded. "You'll be coming down with a case of pneumonia if you don't get inside."

With relief she saw he was dressed again. She managed to slip past him, into the welcome warmth of the cabin. Much as she was beginning to hate the confined, primitive space, the contrast to the wintry scene outside felt almost comforting and cozy. The smell of burning pine and the sound of those crackling logs helped make the room seem cheerful.

"I'm going out to chop down a couple of small trees before it gets dark," Brad announced. "There's plenty of hot water if you want to scrub down while I'm gone." He headed for the door, pausing to add over his shoulder, "I promise I won't peek."

Finding it impossible to look at him, Anne studied the pot on the stove. "I'd appreciate that."

"I thought you would." The door creaked open. "Oh, what I wouldn't give right now for a buzz saw."

She was immediately ashamed of her petty thoughts. He had the tough part, after all—finding wood, dragging it back to the cabin, chopping down trees, chopping it into logs. And he did it all without complaining. For a city guy, he was really pretty capable. The kind of man a woman would be lucky to have around in a crisis. She could forgive his warped sense of humor, she thought, as long as he didn't try any more of his games. She didn't like being permanently off balance when she was around him.

Getting washed all over was a harrowing experience, especially since she had one ear constantly trained on the door, listening for the steady thud of Brad's axe to cease. Every time the sound stopped she froze, then relaxed when it continued. Finally, she was done and dressed again, and ready to face what the next night would bring.

How many more nights would they have to stay there, she wondered, as she peered out the window at the gathering dusk. How her family must be suffering, not knowing what had happened to her. She could even feel sorry for Darlene Irving. Brad was all she had now that her husband was gone. That must be a terrifying feeling, not knowing what had happened to the only member of your family you had left.

The object of her thoughts appeared in front of the window at that moment, his arms loaded with freshly chopped wood. She hurried to open the door for him, grateful for his company again. The isolation was beginning to get her down.

"The sky's clearing again," Brad said, as he dropped the logs with a loud clatter in front of the stove. "We could have a nice day tomorrow."

"Then we should have more chance of being rescued."

He glanced over at her. "If it's clear early enough,

I guess they should be able to spot us and get a ground crew up here.''

"I'm afraid to hope for too much anymore.''

His gaze sharpened. "Don't give up hope, Annie. There's always hope.''

"I know.'' She sat down at the table and propped her chin on her hands. "It's just that we're stuck on this mountain on New Year's Eve, we're running out of food, and we don't even have any wine to toast in the new year.'' She didn't know why she added that last comment. She didn't even want to be awake at midnight.

"Speaking of food, do we have anything for dinner?'' He squatted down in front of the stove and poked at smoldering logs. "I'm getting hungry.''

She scowled at him. "Just like a man. Always thinking about his stomach.''

"It will give us something to do.''

"Well, there's that, I suppose.'' She got to her feet and limped over to the shelves. "I'd better light the lamp. It's getting too dark to see.''

"I'll do it.'' He got to his feet and came over to her. "Where are the matches?''

"Here. I put them in the saucer.'' She gave them to him, and watched him turn up the wick. "There can't be much oil left in it.''

"There's not. I'll turn the wick down low. Once this goes out, we'll have to rely on firelight.''

"Wonderful.'' She reached for a jar. "It will have to be soup and rice again.''

"Sounds delicious. I can hardly wait.''

"Not the dinner we were anticipating at the lodge, is it?''

"Nope, but it's better than eating snow. Which is what we'd be doing by now if we hadn't found the cabin."

His interminable optimism was beginning to irritate her. "Are you always this cheerful, or are you making an effort for my benefit?"

He grinned. "A little bit of both. As I said earlier, we'll get through this if we can both keep a sense of humor. How's the ankle doing, by the way?"

"Better, thanks." She poured some dried soup into a fresh pot of water, and added a handful of rice. "I could probably get down the mountain on it if we could find the way."

"Well, we may have to try if we don't get picked up tomorrow."

It was the first time he'd indicated that they might not be rescued the next day, and it frightened her. She carried the pot to the stove and set it on the hot plate. "If the sky is clear we could keep a sense of direction."

"If it stays clear. You know as well as I do how quickly the storms come in. A whiteout can completely disorient even the most experienced climber. I'd hate to take that chance and end up without proper shelter."

She stirred the soup with one of the plastic spoons. "It might be better to take that chance than starve to death here."

"Well, let's worry about that tomorrow. How do you want to celebrate New Year's Eve?"

"By sleeping through it."

"That's not the answer I was looking for."

She eyed him suspiciously. "So, what do you suggest?"

"I think we should party. Play charades, sing." He looked at her from beneath lowered lashes. "If I remember, my dear, you have a beautiful voice."

"Hey, that wasn't my best effort. I was under a lot of stress."

"Well here's your chance to show me what you can really do."

"Believe me, you're better off not knowing."

"And here I was under the impression that the Parkers excelled at everything."

For some utterly stupid reason, she felt tears pricking her eyelids. "No," she said unsteadily. "Some of us are not very good when it comes to making like a pioneer."

He must have detected something in her tone, as his expression changed at once. "Oh, nuts. I'm sorry. I didn't mean to upset you."

She shook her head at him, feeling stupid yet seemingly unable to stop the flow of tears. "I don't know why I'm crying. I guess it's just everything. Being stranded up here, not knowing if everyone's all right at the lodge, if they're worrying about me, the whole reason I'm here…I mean being back in Grand Springs when I should be in Denver, oh, hell." She laid down the spoon and put her hand over her mouth.

"Aw, Annie, you've been through an awful lot. Don't cry. Just come here."

He held out his hands, and it seemed the most natural thing in the world to go to him. She didn't even think about it until she was enclosed in the musky warmth within the strong circle of his arms, her cheek resting on his chest.

At first she let herself relax, enjoying the reassuring contact of his strength. Then, gradually, she became aware of the nuances of her position. The soft, furry texture of his sweater against her cheek, the steady thud of his heartbeat beneath her ear, the powerful pressure of his forearms clamped hard around her.

His fingers stirred in the small of her back, and a shock of awareness trembled from the subtle movement all the way down to her toes.

Not Brad Irving. She couldn't possibly want this man—her family's sworn enemy, playboy of the month, breaker of hearts. She had to be crazy. Or just plain stupid. Or both. Whatever it was, there was no mistaking that sensation that tightened somewhere deep in her belly and spread rapidly down in a ripple of fire.

Determined to fight her body's treacherous needs, she pulled away from him. Or at least, she attempted to, but he held her fast, resisting her efforts to free herself from his provocative embrace. She looked up, and knew the minute she did that she'd made a bad mistake.

His intent expression fanned the heat already clouding her senses. She knew, without a doubt, that he was about to kiss her. And this time there would be no helicopter to interrupt. Somewhere in the fast fading recesses of her mind, she was absolutely certain that if she let this happen now, if she gave him this one small victory, he would want more. He wasn't the kind of man to be satisfied with a kiss, not with that furnace of desire smoldering in his eyes. For the space of a heartbeat, she thought about resisting, but then his mouth descended hard on hers, and that thought was wiped from her mind.

She put everything she had into that kiss. All her frustrations, all her fears, all her disappointments, all her self-doubts, every emotion she'd ever experienced seemed to dissolve and merge into one, single, ecstatic response.

The embers that had been smoldering between them ever since they'd entered that cabin suddenly exploded into a roaring heat. His mouth was hungry on hers, searching, demanding, exploring, while his hands trailed paths of fire up and down her body. His beard softly scraped her chin, but the sensation only added to her excitement.

With his hands on her hips, he dragged her closer, letting her know just how badly he wanted her. The contact of his hard arousal sent waves of excitement screeching through every nerve in her trembling body.

Never mind who he was, what he was. She was answering a call now that was far beyond coherent thought or rationalization. He was man and she was woman, he was hot and she was on fire, and there was only one way either one of them was going to satisfy that terrible, exquisite ache of need.

She tore at his clothes, and feverishly helped him drag off her own—wanting, needing the touch of his naked body against hers. He paused, just briefly, pulling back to gaze at her exposed breasts, his expression almost reverent as he consumed her with his hungry eyes.

Helpless and trembling, she stood bathed in the heat of that burning gaze, every inch of her flesh craving him, every nerve twisted tight in anticipation. Her nipples ached for his touch, and when he finally, carefully, stretched out his hand and gently stroked the undercurve of her breast with the back of his index finger, her knees buckled. Slowly he moved his finger over her hardened nipple, and a small sound of pleasure escaped her parted lips.

"Damn, Annie, you are beautiful."

Swallowing hard, she lowered her gaze down his flat stomach and over his belly to his thighs. She had to moisten her dry lips with her tongue before she could answer him. "So are you," she whispered.

"I want you so much. So damn much it hurts."

She smiled, empowered by the knowledge. "Then what are we waiting for?"

With a guttural sound that thrilled her to the core, he reached for her and buried his mouth in her neck. She clung to him, stroking everywhere she could reach, until the need coiling inside her became so intense she was close to begging for release.

Just when she thought she could stand his searing touch no longer, he swept her up in his arms and lowered her onto the cot. He took barely a second or two to gaze on her one last time, then sprawled across her, his mouth hunting, finding and tasting every inch of her craving body.

The world disappeared, the walls fading in the haze of sheer, intense excitement of mind and flesh. Wave after wave of excruciating pleasure almost overwhelmed her, her mind shattered by the intensity of her response to his expert touch. Induced by his gentle but persistent fingers, her release came suddenly, furiously, incredibly beautiful and bringing her close to tears.

So gratified was she that the urge to give back, to give him the pleasure he'd given her, was uncontrollable. Never in her life had she felt such passion, such a fierce need to satisfy this incredible man who had led her through a door she had never known was there.

She thrust him onto his back, almost throwing them both off the bed in her eagerness. His throaty laugh excited her, challenged her. She wanted him writhing and helpless beneath her as she had been with him. Instinct guided her as she experimented, with her hands and her tongue, until his groans warned her he was close to breaking.

Finally, he'd had enough. "Come here, you seductive witch," he growled, and hauled her up his body until she was straddled across his hips. He found her, hard and fast, and his sudden, fierce intrusion sent her off on another wave of ecstacy.

Still joined together, he rolled her over, shifting and sliding her body under him until they were centered on the narrow cot. She ran shivering hands down the curve of his back bone to the swell of his buttocks, while his hips slowly undulated back and forth, with a sensuous rhythm that powered the craving all over again.

Faster and faster he stroked, back and forth, while she clasped his hips with her thighs, tighter and tighter, and her world flashed by her in an explosion of light and dark. This time he joined her, soaring on an unforgettable high that took them beyond coherent thought, and then gently floated them back to earth, to the cot, to the cabin, to reality.

He lay for a long time, half resting on her body, his arm heavy on her stomach. Thoughts crowded her mind, jostling for space, insistent on being heard. The cabin seemed awfully warm, and the smell of wood smoke seemed a little more acrid than usual. She wondered if it had started snowing again. She wondered if the lodge had escaped damage from the avalanche and everyone was celebrating the new year in as planned. Though she doubted her family would be celebrating anything.

Finally she allowed the thoughts she'd been avoiding to infiltrate her mind. She'd just made love with the one man in the world she should have avoided at all costs. If her father knew what she had done, he'd probably take a shotgun to Brad's head. If her mother knew what she'd done, she'd more than likely disown her. Banish her from the family. If her sisters knew what she'd done, they'd probably want all the details.

In spite of her reservations, Anne had to smile at the thought. Her smile faded, however, when she considered the consequences of what she'd done. She'd stopped taking the Pill after Jason had left, convinced she would never again get involved with a man. She certainly hadn't expected to be in this situation.

She vaguely remembered Brad muttering about protection, and the fact he hadn't brought any with him. Obviously he hadn't expected this either. Under the circumstances they'd both taken a pretty potent risk. Carried away by the moment, it hadn't seemed that important at the time. Now she'd have to worry about it for at least another week or two.

She should resent him for that, but she couldn't. Not right now, anyway. Not while she was feeling so wonderfully satisfied and content, like a stray cat who had suddenly found a home. She turned her head and looked at the face of the man who had just consumed her in a blazing inferno of passion.

His eyes were closed, his expression relaxed and at peace. With his hair mussed and jaw unshaved, he looked rugged, primitive and definitely dangerous. How could she have fallen for a man like this?

In that instant he opened his eyes, and smiled at her. "Hi, beautiful."

His voice was husky, contented—the voice of a man who'd just waged a tough battle and won. The voice of exhaustion and sheer indulgence.

She pulled a face at him. "Where's all this marvelous stamina you keep bragging about? You look as if you're ready to go to sleep."

His lazy grin made her want to kiss him again. "What do you want me to do? Strut around like a baboon beating my chest?"

She thought about it. "Something like that. Some indication that you enjoyed it as much as I did."

He closed one eye. "Ah, is that what all this is about? Well, sweetheart, there are more ways than one to demonstrate how much I enjoyed making love to you. Give me a little time to catch my breath and I'll give you a repeat performance."

"You're kidding."

"Try me." His grin turned wicked.

She was about to answer him when she finally identified the odd smell she'd noticed earlier. She uttered a soft squeak. "The soup! It's burning." Without thinking about it she leapt from the bed and hobbled over to the stove. The handle of the pot was red-hot to the touch, and she had to grab up her sweater from the floor and use it as a pot holder.

When she'd finally shifted the pot far enough away from the hot plate, she lifted the lid, wrinkling her nose at the smell of burned food. Quickly she stirred the soup, and little bits of browned vegetables and rice appeared in the mixture. "Drat," she muttered. "Now look what you made me do."

She glanced over at Brad, and was disconcerted to see him propped up on one elbow, watching her with a look of pure delight on his face. In an effort to cover her confusion and sudden self-consciousness, she said crossly, "It's not a laughing matter, Brad. This is the last of the soup. And now I've burned it."

"It wouldn't be the first time I've eaten burned food, and I don't suppose it will be the last."

"Maybe not," Anne said dismally. "But when it's all you have to eat and you don't have any other choice—"

"If it's all we have to eat then it doesn't matter what it tastes like. It's better than the alternative."

"I suppose so. But I did want it to be at least edible. It's our New Year's Eve dinner."

"Tell you what. When we get back to town I'll take you out to dinner to make up for it."

She stopped stirring and laid the spoon down. His words had given her a cold feeling in her stomach. She didn't want to think about getting back to town now, she realized. That was a different world away, and one she would have to face sooner or later. But right now, right this moment, all she wanted was to stay secure and warm in this cramped, primitive, ugly little cabin that somewhere in the last hour or so they'd managed to turn into something very special.

"I'll tell you something else," Brad went on, when she didn't answer him. "Burned soup or not, how bad could it possibly taste when it's being fixed by a beautiful, sexy angel in the nude? Do you always cook that way? If so, you're going to have a regular visitor for meals."

She made a face at him. "You won't get any of this if you don't behave. Get up and get dressed, and we'll eat it before it gets any worse than it is."

He groaned and flung himself on his back. "Why do women always have to be so practical?"

"Because women are responsible for the perpetuation of the species. If it were left to men, we'd still be running around in loin cloths wielding axes and hunting for food."

"Hmm...I think I'd like that. Women dressed in loin cloths, waiting impatiently for the big, macho hunter to come home and service them."

"You are disgusting." She launched herself with her good foot and made a flying leap for the bed, ignoring his grunt of protest when she landed on him. "Now get up you smug, self-satisfied little hedonist and eat dinner." She nuzzled his neck with her nose. "I've slaved all day over a hot stove for you."

Clamping his arms around her, he muttered, "Not until you take back those harsh words and give me some sweet talk."

"If I give you the slightest bit of encouragement, Mister, we'll be eating cold soup."

His mouth traveled down her neck to the hollow in

her throat. His lips tickled her skin as he murmured, "Yeah? So what's wrong with that?"

She couldn't believe the heat was there again, boiling up inside her. She wriggled free, and climbed off him, before she could give in to the temptation. "There's only one thing worse than burned soup," she said, bending down to pick up clothes, "and that's cold burned soup. So move it, lover boy, or I'll eat your share as well as mine."

She flung his clothes on the bed, then hastily pulled on her own. Maybe this was wrong, she thought, as she hurried back to the stove. Maybe she'd live to regret this night. But she'd worry about that later. Right now, she was enjoying this moment in time, this weird and wonderful New Year's Eve. And it wasn't even over yet.

Chapter 7

There was no champagne cooling on ice at the table that night. There was no tiger prawn cocktail, no Caesar salad, no steak and lobster, no baked Alaska, no noisemakers and silly hats. There were only the two of them, immersed in the cozy warmth of the crackling, snapping fire and each other. It was the most magical, meaningful New Year's Eve Brad had ever experienced. In the thirty-six hours since he'd pulled Annie from the ravine, his life had been changed forever.

It didn't matter that the soup was burned, or that the water tasted flat. All that mattered was the woman facing him across the rickety old table, her silky hair tumbled about her lovely face, a world of promise in her incredible green eyes and a laugh that could make his insides melt. He was as drunk on her magnetism as if he had consumed an entire bottle of the best champagne.

If someone had ever told him he could feel like this about a woman he'd have laughed in their face. If someone had told him that woman would be Annie Parker, he'd have had them certified insane. He still couldn't believe it himself.

Annie Parker was everything a woman should be. Beautiful, funny, intelligent and sexy as hell. Somewhere deep in his gut he knew that it couldn't be as simple as that. There would be a price to pay for this night. There always was. Sooner or later he would have to forget the fantasy and face the realities. Right now, this minute, the night and this woman were his to enjoy. And he was going to make the most of it all while he could.

He would sing to her, dance with her, play charades with her, and in the waning hours of the old year, he would make love to her again. Only this time he'd have the luxury of taking things slowly, savoring each moment as he watched her desire build until she exploded the way she had earlier.

He'd suspected she was capable of intense passion. In his wildest dreams he could never have imagined the tremendous power of her touch, the almost unbearable excitement of sinking into her warm, smooth flesh and bringing her to fulfillment. She was all woman, and she had made him feel more of a man than anyone or anything had ever managed to do in the past.

He could hardly wait to begin again the slow, exquisite ritual of raw lovemaking at its best. But he needed to be patient. He wanted her to enjoy it all as much as he did, and he wanted to give her the romance, the tenderness, the quiet joy of sharing a truly beautiful experience. He wanted to give her the moon, all wrapped up in a star-studded night of love. And never, never in his life had he ever felt this way before.

He helped her rinse off the dishes, standing behind her, his arms around her while they splashed cold water over the faded plastic plates. He hummed love tunes while he danced with her across the splintered floor, carefully protecting her injured ankle.

He played charades, and when it was his turn, he parodied the title of a song—a love song that had haunted the radio waves since last summer. When she finally guessed it, he took her fingers, pressed them to his lips and then his heart.

Her eyes grew soft, then slowly heated as he drew her close, and barely brushed her lips with his. "I want you," he whispered.

"I want you, too."

Just simple words, but, oh, how they made his heart sing. He took her hand and drew her to the cot. Carefully he undressed her trembling body, then lowered her gently down. She watched him take off his clothes, and never in his life had he felt such an erotic sensation as her warm gaze on his naked body.

He made himself take time, making each intimate movement as pleasurable as he could for her. He was rewarded again and again as her murmurs turned to cries of agonized pleasure. He couldn't get enough of her body writhing and arching at his touch. Her fierce kisses thrilled him, the sharp pain of her nails digging into his back excited him beyond reason. Finally, at long last, when he could stand the agony no more, he took her, forcing himself to hold back with slow, languid thrusts until her body convulsed in a frenzy of need.

He felt as if he were flying head-on into a tornado, spinning him around in a searing vortex of passion. His soul sang with triumph, while his heart melted at the precious gift she was giving him. Time ceased to have any meaning, life itself faded into insignificance as all his energy, his thoughts and his emotions centered on one magnificent entity—the sharing of something so breathtaking it defied imagination.

Dimly he was aware of her cries as together they fought for release, then he was there, riding the highest wave of his life as he emptied his seed inside her. Gradually the world settled down again, and he collapsed, his energy spent. At last, he was at peace.

Anne lay for a long time, listening to the steady rhythm of his breathing as he slept. The fire in the woodstove gradually burned down, and the crackling ceased, leaving the cabin basking in the deep silence of the snow-covered mountains.

Her body still tingled, her mind felt numb. What she had just experienced was beyond description. This was the way lovemaking should be—wild and primitive, freely and utterly selfless. Two people giving their all, and taking just as passionately with every fiber of their being, every shred of their soul.

She wondered how rare that was—two people so in tune with each other that their minds were joined just as completely as their bodies. It seemed as if they had been destined for this night, ever since her magnificent Viking had towered over her in the school yard of Pike Elementary.

"I hate you, Bradley Irving. I hate you."

"Yeah? Well, I hate you, too, Annie Parker. So that makes us even."

She smiled in the darkness, the memory of those childhood voices floating in her mind. Such a thin line between love and hate. Even then, she hadn't wanted to hate him. Even though she was supposed to despise him and everything he stood for. Even though her loyalty to her family had kept her from admitting the truth. That to her, Brad Irving had always been that tall, powerful Viking with eyes that could destroy her soul. And whose touch, she knew now, could open the door to paradise.

She slept, waking with every subtle movement he made, absorbing the feel of his nakedness against her bare flesh, immersing herself in the warm, male smell of his body.

When he woke her again, his lips softly pressed to hers, it was from a deep sleep. "Sorry," he murmured, when she opened her eyes. "Just couldn't resist."

She smiled sleepily at him, luxuriating in a feeling of such contentment, she felt like purring. "Happy New Year," she said softly.

He kissed her again, more firmly this time. "Happy New Year to you, too."

It was light, she noticed. Bright light. In fact, the whole room was alive with dancing sunbeams. Her stomach leapt as she realized the significance of that. "It looks as if we have a clear day."

He grinned, and she watched the tiny lines form at

the corners of his mouth, fascinated by the spectacle. "We do, indeed, princess. The clouds have gone, the sky is blue and the world is ours."

"It's cold in here."

"I know." He gathered her close, holding her fast against his chest, his soft hair tickling her cheek. "I'll light the fire. In a minute. Just as soon as I've—" He broke off, his body stiffening. "What's that?"

She felt a spasm of apprehension. "What? I can't hear anything."

"Listen." He let her go and sat up. "There! Can you hear it now?"

She sat up, too, dragging the tattered blanket up to cover her breasts. The dull growl in the distance was so faint she thought at first it might be the wind in the stovepipe. But then, as she listened, the sound grew louder. "It's an engine." She stared at him, her eyes wide with hope. "Helicopter? We have to signal."

Brad shook his head. "No, it's too consistent to be a helicopter. I think it's a snowplow. Could even be two of them." He leapt from the bed and padded across the floor to the window.

For a moment or two she was distracted by the fluent lines of his naked body, but then he turned to look at her, and his words obliterated her shameless thoughts. "Our rescuers have arrived. Judging by the speed they're approaching, I'd say they should be here any minute."

The real world, with all its implications came crashing into her sacred haven. "No! They can't find us here like this!" She flung the blanket aside, and dived for her clothes. "Get dressed, Brad. For heaven's sake get your clothes on."

He sauntered across to her, maddening her with his lack of concern. "Annie? Are you trying to tell me that our honeymoon's over?"

She scowled up at him, increasingly conscious of the roar of the snowplows drawing closer. "Bradley Irving, so help me, if you don't get dressed this instant I'll—" She choked off the threat as the roar shut off abruptly, followed by the echo of someone shouting.

The voice was too far away to understand the words, but close enough for the owner to arrive at the door any second. Brad pulled a face. "That was fast."

Fully dressed now, Anne headed for the door. "I'll stall them long enough for you to get your clothes on."

"I'm right behind you."

Hoping he meant what he said, she pulled open the door and limped out onto the landing.

Brad had been right about the snowplows. They sat side by side, a man at each wheel and two more climbing down to the ground. The sun almost blinded her, and she shaded her eyes with one hand and waved with the other.

"Ms. Parker? Is that you?"

Anne vaguely recognized the man heading toward the cabin. He worked for her father's construction company. Her heart leapt, then dropped, then started beating way too fast when she recognized the man behind him staggering through the dense drifts.

She almost fell down the steps in her hurry to get to him. He stopped when he saw her, then held out his arms. She fell into them, half laughing and half crying. When she could get her breath again she pulled out of his fierce bear hug and grinned at him. "Hi, Daddy," she said unsteadily.

He grinned back, though the haggard lines of strain on his face betrayed his anguish. "Hi, Kitten. You had us all pretty worried. Your mother hasn't slept in two nights."

The other man had gone back to the snowplow. She could hear someone talking into a radio and the crackling of an answering voice. It all seemed so unreal. Her father had appeared here on this mountain, as if he'd stepped right into one of her dreams.

Dan Parker still held on to her as if afraid to let her go, and she hugged his arm. "I'm all right, Daddy. What about Elise and Sharon, and Paul? Did they make it down safely?"

Dan nodded, his eyes misting up. "All safe and sound," he said, his voice breaking. "Thank God I have all of my family back now."

She felt terrible, knowing how everyone must have suffered, while she had just spent the most incredible night of her life. "How's Mom holding up? And Gramps?"

Dan Parker pulled a face. "You know Dad. Takes everything as it comes. He never doubted for one minute that you were safe and would come back to us. He even—" Dan's face darkened. "What the hell is *he* doing here?"

With a pang of apprehension, Anne swung around to follow his gaze. Brad stood in the doorway watching them, his expression wary.

"Brad rescued me from a ravine." Anne turned

back to face her father. "He was wonderful. I would have died if he hadn't pulled me out of there. He found the cabin and helped me up here and—"

"He's been here with you all the time?"

Anne felt her cheeks warm. "If it hadn't been for Brad, I would have frozen to death. He chopped down trees to make a fire—"

"Spare me the gruesome details." Dan's face looked like thunder. "Get on the plow, Anne. Your mother is waiting for you."

"You could at least thank him," Anne said quietly. "He saved my life."

Dan's mouth tightened. "If he did there had to be an ulterior motive. An Irving never did anything unless he could profit by it. Now get on the plow. It isn't fair to keep your mother waiting any longer."

"I'm not going anywhere until I say goodbye." She pulled out of her father's grasp and hobbled back to the cabin steps.

Brad stared silently down at her, his face inscrutable.

"I'm sorry." The ache in her throat made talking difficult and she swallowed. "I'll call you."

His mouth twitched in a semblance of his grin. "Sure you will."

"I promise."

"Irving," Dan Parker snapped from behind her. "Don't think this gives you any claims as far as my daughter is concerned."

Embarrassed, Anne turned on her father. "I'm quite capable of handling my own life, thank you. I'm not a child anymore."

"Then stop behaving like one."

Before Anne could answer him, Brad interrupted, his voice as cutting as the wind-driven snow. "You have nothing to worry about, *Mr.* Parker. I'm no threat to your daughter. We're just ships that passed in the night. There's nothing more to it than that."

The words seemed to stab, one by one, into her soul. "Come on, Daddy," she said quietly. "Let's go home."

To her relief, he moved off with her, following her over to the plow. She climbed up into the seat, and the second she was seated the man behind the wheel fired the engine. With a roar and a spray of snow, the plow turned, and Brad disappeared from view.

Her father, perched behind her on the tow bar, barely spoke to her on the way down. The driver of the snowplow, a young man with a full beard and sharp eyes, fired a barrage of questions at her, which she did her best to answer. Conscious of her father listening, she skipped over the part that Brad played in the adventure, and concentrated instead on her own feelings and concerns.

According to the driver, the helicopter had spotted the smoke from the cabin when it had flown over the day before, but had been unable to land. The pilot had alerted the lodge, however, and once the plows had cleared the road they'd headed out at first light to find the cabin.

When the lodge finally came into view, Anne gasped at the sight of torn walls, sagging roof and smashed windows. The porch had completely disappeared beneath a massive mound of snow, which almost reached the roof on one side.

"Was anyone hurt?" she asked anxiously, as the

plow roared to a stop in front of what had once been the main entrance.

"A lot of people," Dan said grimly, as he helped his daughter down to the ground. "The Petrocellis are here though, and they've been taking care of everyone. They got the road open last night and ambulances took the injured down to Vanderbilt. Luckily none of them were hurt seriously."

"Anyone we know?" She didn't want to mention Darlene Irving, but she knew how devastated Brad would be if anything happened to his mother.

Her father rattled off a list of names, but Anne barely paid attention. The second snowplow had just arrived, and she wanted to get her father inside the ruins of the lodge before he had a chance to say something nasty to Brad.

Inside the ballroom, her entire family waited to greet her with smiles, jokes and hugs. Carol Parker burst into tears at the sight of her daughter, and Anne's own eyes misted up as she hugged everyone. Even Grandpa James looked as if he might want to blow his nose.

"There's Brad Irving!" Sharon said, interrupting Paul's rapid-fire questions with a wave of her hand. "They must have found him, too."

"He was with me," Anne said, avoiding her father's baleful look. "He rescued me from a ravine and saved my life."

Sharon's eyes grew wide. "He was with you the whole time?"

Elise chimed in with disbelief in her voice. "In the cabin? For two nights?"

Grandpa James whistled softly when Anne nodded.

"Oh, Anne," her mother said brokenly. "That must have been dreadful for you."

"It wasn't easy," Anne said carefully, "but we managed to survive without killing each other."

"He didn't try anything, did he?" Paul demanded, glaring across the room to where Brad was encased in Darlene's arms.

"Of course not." Anne crossed her fingers behind her back. "We were much too busy trying to stay alive."

Elise and Sharon looked at each other with disappointment written all over their faces.

"What a terrible experience, dear." Her mother touched her arm. "Truly awful. Why are you limping? Did you hurt your ankle?"

Thankful for the change of focus, Anne again recounted her adventure, mentioning Brad as little as possible. Although she did her best not to look at him, she knew the moment he turned to leave, and caught the searching glance he sent her way before disappearing from sight with his mother.

In spite of her overwhelming relief and joy to be back in civilization once again, she knew she would never forget those stolen moments in a snowbound cabin, with a man who could turn her world on its side with one touch of his hand.

The first thing Anne did when she arrived home was head for the shower and some clean clothes. Her sisters followed her everywhere, asking a dozen questions about Brad that she either couldn't, or was determined not to, answer. Her father kept muttering vague threats every time Brad's name was mentioned, and her mother cornered her at every opportunity, asking hopefully if there was anything Anne wanted to tell her.

With her family surrounding her, her hunger sated by the huge brunch her mother prepared, and the cozy warmth of her family's living room, Anne did her best to appreciate the comparative luxury. The memories kept intruding, however, as she knew they would.

She did her best to focus on the present, and forget the past. Everything still looked the same as it had two days ago, yet she couldn't escape the feeling that something had changed, irrevocably, and that nothing would ever be quite the same again.

She glanced across the room at Grandpa James, dozing in his armchair in the corner by the bookcases. His straggly white beard rested on his chest, and he snored quietly amidst her sisters' chatter. He was the only one, she realized, who hadn't acted as if she'd been victimized in some way.

Elise and Sharon had challenged Paul to a Monopoly game, while her father had buried his face behind a newspaper, his feet up on the footstool her mother had cross-stitched with such care one long, cold winter.

The Christmas tree still stood in the corner of the room, looking a little forlorn without the pile of gifts beneath it, in spite of its colorful ornaments and tinsel. The flames leapt and danced in the grate, snapping, crackling and sending up blue sparks every now and again.

They reminded her of the woodstove in the cabin. She could still hear the spitting and hissing sound the logs made, while she lay in the dark, clasped in the peaceful warmth of Brad's arms.

She missed him, she realized, staring into the flames. She missed his teasing, his dry humor, the way his eyebrows twitched when he was provoked. She missed his voice, low and husky, telling her that she was beautiful. No one had ever called her beautiful in quite that tone of voice before.

She missed the searing touch of his hands, the rough texture of his bare legs entwined with hers. She even missed the drafty, shabby cabin, with its dusty windows and creaking floor.

She was being such a fool. In spite of everything she knew about him, she'd fallen for that old line. She'd become one of Brad Irving's casual affairs. And now it was over. She would have to go on with her life, waiting for him to parade a new conquest around town. The thought was unbearable.

Maybe she should leave again. Go back to Denver. Or find somewhere else to start over. Even as the idea formed in her mind, she knew she couldn't give in to it. She'd run away once, from Denver, after Jason had betrayed her. She couldn't keep running away from her problems. She had to face them.

She looked up, to find Grandpa James staring at her from across the room. His expression was grave, and she wondered for an instant if he could read her thoughts. She smiled at him to dispel the odd notion. He didn't smile back, just nodded at her, and closed his eyes again.

She slept badly that night, and the next. Her bed had never felt so lonely, so cold and empty. She kept wondering what he was doing, who he was with, if he was thinking about her with the same aching loneliness that the memories brought her.

She knew it was wishful thinking. Men like Brad Irving didn't waste time on memories. They made the most of the moment, then moved on, without ever looking back. And she must do the same. She had promised to call. But that was before he'd looked her father straight in the eye and uttered those cold, meaningless words. *We're just ships that passed in the night. There's nothing more to it than that.*

There was no point in calling him. That could only prolong the inevitable. "Happy New Year, Annie," she whispered into the dark empty room. And wept.

Across town in his comfortable apartment, Brad lay with his hands behind his head, staring into the darkness of the cold night. He hadn't been able to stop thinking about Annie since he'd seen her leave with her father.

He knew she wouldn't call. Her family was too important to her. He remembered how worried she'd been about them, how concerned for their fears for her safety. He remembered how her face lit up whenever she mentioned any of them, and he would never forget that scene in the snow outside the cabin, when she'd flung herself into her father's arms.

Annie had been out of town too long. She'd forgotten the times he'd been slighted by her family. Ignored in public, talked about in private, all his life he'd had to deal with hostility from the Parkers—a hostility that had been generated by people who weren't even alive when he was born. Annie herself had been governed by that resentment, at least until now.

His own father had immortalized the damn feud, refusing to sell the resort and the land with it for the sole purpose of keeping it out of Parker hands. He'd died to keep it, and now the land sat, empty and abandoned, a visual bone of contention to everyone who passed it by.

Brad rolled onto his side and pulled the comforter over his shoulder. He'd closed down the spa because he couldn't bear what it stood for. He'd refused to work with his father, causing them both pain, because of what that business represented. And now he couldn't do anything with it at all, because no matter what he did, the Parkers would claim he was using their land, stolen from them decades ago. He wasn't about to be drawn into their silly quarrel.

But none of this mattered when it came to Annie. It was ironic that she should be part of the family who had taken away his self-respect, to the point where he had deliberately perpetuated the image they had painted of him. Maybe he'd even believed he *was* that frivolous, irresponsible playboy who found it so impossible to settle down. His father certainly had believed it. The whole town believed it.

Brad smiled ruefully in the darkness. Annie could have changed all that. With her love, her laughter and her compassion, she could have given him back what her family had taken away. His belief in himself.

For the first time in his life, he wanted to hang on to a relationship with both hands and all of his heart. For the first time in his life, he was afraid that if he didn't hang on to this woman, that if he let her go, he would never be happy again.

He needed her, in a way he'd never needed anything or anyone before. He needed her as much as he needed to breathe. He needed her warmth, her compassion, her funny little laugh, her wonderful, exciting passion and her incredible body. He wanted her quiet sympathy, her quick understanding and her bright, intelligent mind. He wanted her in every way a man wants a woman, without conditions or promises or reservations.

He lifted his head and pummeled the pillow with his fist. He couldn't just let her slip away. He couldn't allow an ancient feud and misguided people to stand in the way of what could be the best thing that had happened to him in his life.

He had to try. He would find a way to see her again and together they would find out if they had something real going on between them. Though he was very much afraid that if he did, some people were going to get hurt. It was unavoidable. He just hoped it wouldn't be Annie.

Chapter 8

"It's time I started looking for an apartment," Anne announced at the breakfast table a few days later. "I need to find an office to lease and get back to work."

"We'll help," Elise said, nudging Sharon in the shoulder. "It'll be fun."

"You know you're welcome to stay here as long as you want," Carol murmured. She handed a plate of hotcakes over to Grandpa James. "There's plenty of room. When Sharon and Elise go back to college this house seems so empty. I keep telling your father, once the girls move out we'll have to get rid of it. It's just too big for the two of us."

"Then we're never moving out." Elise looked at her sister for support.

"We will when we get married," Sharon said, helping herself to some scrambled eggs. "You don't really want to bring up babies in this relic of antiquity, do you?''

Carol looked offended. "It was good enough for all of you.''

"That was then. I'm talking about now. They have some lovely houses down by the lake.''

"Lovely prices, too," Grandpa James muttered. "Don't know why they can't build houses cheaper. Don't see how anyone can afford a house nowadays.''

Elise laughed. "Sharon thinks she's going to meet a really rich man, who'll marry her and buy her a fancy house by the lake, and a boat, and she'll never have to worry about money again.''

"So what?" Sharon furiously buttered her toast. "It's not that impossible.''

Grandpa James nodded. "Aim high, that's what I always say.''

"Well, maybe you should go after Brad Irving, then," Elise said, sending Anne a sly look. "He's got pots of money, and he's good-looking as well. What do you think, Anne?''

"I never really noticed," Anne said casually.

"How could you *not* notice? You were with him for two whole nights.''

"I wasn't thinking about his looks." She was getting too good at telling lies, she thought uneasily. "Or his money," she added. At least that much was the truth. She looked across the table at Grandpa James, who seemed intent on pouring syrup on his hotcakes. "You're right about the price of houses, Gramps. I noticed how much they'd gone up since I left.''

Her ruse to change the subject worked. Her mother and sisters all leapt into the discussion, with Carol warning her daughters that none of them would ever afford to buy a house unless they started saving right now.

"It's the older people who suffer," Grandpa James said, waving his fork at the rest of them. "Some of these widows can't afford to pay their mortgage and taxes, and can't afford the rent for a decent place to live. It's a shame. Worked all their dang lives and have to live in poverty just when they should be sitting back and enjoying life."

The phone rang just then, putting an effective end to the discussion. Elise rushed to answer it, and came back with her face flushed with excitement. "It's for you," she said, smirking at Anne. "It's Brad Irving."

"Oh, my." Carol put her hand to her throat. "Thank goodness your father and Paul have gone to work."

"Yeah, Dad would have had a coronary if he'd been here." Elise laughed. "Aren't you going to talk to him, Anne? He'll get tired of waiting."

Anne pushed her chair back and dropped her napkin on the table. Her heart thudded so hard against her ribs she felt sure everyone in the room could hear it. "Excuse me," she muttered. "I'll take it in my room." She escaped from the speculative glances of her family and hurried up the stairs. Damn him. And damn her own treacherous heart for caring so much.

Inside the sanctuary of her room, she took a few deep breaths to calm her nerves, then picked up the phone. Her greeting was answered immediately by Brad's deep voice.

"Hi, how's the ankle?"

She made herself speak slowly and calmly, though

the phone trembled against her ear. "Much better, thanks."

"Sorry to call you there, but I didn't know how else to get hold of you. Hope I didn't cause too much of a sensation."

"None at all. How are you, Brad?"

Apparently she succeeded in her attempt to sound indifferent. There was a short pause before he answered. "Something's come up you might be interested in. An office to lease on Bradford Drive. I know you were looking for one, so I called the lease office and asked them to hold it until you'd had a chance to check it out."

She knew, by the cutting disappointment, that she'd been hoping he'd had a more personal reason to call. She was being such a fool. The knowledge chilled her voice even more. "That was so nice of you to think of me, Brad. I appreciate it. Could you give me the address?"

"Sure. When do you think you could get there? An office in that location is not going to be available for long. Marie, the leasing agent, said she can only hold it until tomorrow."

"I'll go down there this morning." She hunted for a pen, trying very hard not to wonder just how personally he knew this Marie person. Scribbling down the number on the edge of the magazine she'd been reading the night before, she thanked him for letting her know about the lease, and hung up.

When she returned to the dining room, four pairs of eyes gazed expectantly at her face. "Well?" Elise demanded. "What did he want?"

"That's none of our business, dear," Carol murmured, though Anne could tell she was bursting with curiosity.

"It's no big secret," she said hurriedly, before her sisters could start speculating aloud. "Brad heard about an office on Bradford Drive, and passed it along to me. I happened to mention I was looking for one when we were in the cabin."

"I bet that wasn't all you mentioned," Elise murmured. "I wonder what his mother said when she found out you two spent two nights together."

"Elise!" Carol frowned at her youngest daughter. "That's quite enough of that kind of talk. If your father heard you he'd get all upset and you know he has to watch his blood pressure. Besides, you should know by now that Anne would never be personally interested in Brad Irving. She has far too much sense and self-respect. I wish you and Sharon would take a lesson from her."

Sharon looked up with an injured air. "What did *I* do?"

"Nothing, dear. I just think you and Elise have far better things to do than discuss the personal lives of the Irvings, not to mention everyone else in town." She turned to Anne. "Would you like me to go with you this morning? We could look at the office and have lunch afterward."

"Can I come?"

"I'd like to go, too!"

Even Grandpa James looked at her hopefully, Anne noticed. "I'm sorry," she said firmly. "I would rather do this myself. I'll tell you all what it's like when I get back."

She hurried out of the room to get ready, trying not

to feel guilty about depriving her family of an outing. The last thing she needed was her mother pointing out every little drawback to the office, and her sisters poking fun at everything.

Driving down the familiar streets a little later, some of Anne's depression lifted at the thought of working right here in her hometown. There was something comforting about it, a feeling of security, a sense of belonging that she'd never felt while she was in Denver.

Maybe what happened with Jason had been for the best after all. Maybe what she had considered a disaster at the time had really been a blessing, bringing her home again. The door that had opened as another one closed. The chance to start again, and really do something for the town she loved.

She felt a sense of excitement as she parked the car. New opportunities were always an adventure, and one never knew what was around the corner. In fact, if it hadn't been for the thought of bumping into Brad now and again, she would have been utterly content with her new beginning.

The office looked perfect from the outside. Square windows looking out onto the street, and a clean, uncluttered entrance with a small frosted window in the door. The name above the windows had been painted out, but Anne vaguely remembered it as a travel agent's office.

As she climbed out of the car, the door on the driver's side of the car in front opened, and a small, dark-haired woman climbed out. She introduced herself as Marie Westlake, and led Anne into the now abandoned office.

"The lease is very reasonable, considering the location," she told Anne. "This will be snapped up in no time."

Anne had to agree. All she'd need was a couple of desks and cabinets, and she'd be in business. "I'll take it." She smiled at Marie. "Where do I sign?"

Marie laid out the contract on the built-in counter at the rear of the office, and left Anne to read it while she went to make a call from her car.

Anne scanned the familiar lines, pausing now and again to check out a small detail. It was straightforward enough, giving her a two-year lease. Two years, she thought, scrambling in her purse for a pen. A lot could happen in two years.

She heard the door open behind her. With her gaze still focused on the tiny wording in the contract, she called out, "Do you have a pen I could borrow? I can't seem to find mine."

"Which is just as well," a deep voice answered her. "Didn't anyone ever tell you that you should never sign a contract without consulting a lawyer?"

Her breath froze in her throat, and it took her a moment to compose herself enough to turn around and face him. "Brad! How nice of you to stop by."

Something flickered in his eyes, then was gone. "I thought, since I was the one who recommended the office, I should at least take a look at the lease for you. Just in case there are any nasty little hidden clauses that could cost you money."

She managed a light laugh. "I've looked it over pretty thoroughly. There doesn't seem to be anything in there, but you're welcome to look at it, if you want."

He held out his hand for the contract and she gave it to him, uncomfortably aware of the pages fluttering in her nervous fingers. The dark suit he wore made him look taller, giving him a sleek elegance that was so unsettling. The easygoing man in the ski pants and sweater, with his hair mussed and a two-day beard, seemed to have been left behind in that lonely cabin in the mountains.

"Hmm," Brad murmured, scanning the lines of the contract, "everything seems in order. You might want to question the option here." He indicated the paragraph with his forefinger.

She leaned in closer to read the small print, and inadvertently brushed his arm with her breast. She froze at the contact, and stared hard at the wording that had blurred in front of her. His cologne reminded her sharply of that first night in the cabin, lying so close to him in that narrow cot and trying desperately to keep some space between them.

Close on the heels of that memory came another one. His naked body, powerful and demanding in his urgency, exciting her beyond reason.

She fought to banish the erotic images from her mind, and hunted for something to say. Anything that would break the tense silence that seemed to envelop them in its intimate embrace. "Is there a problem?" she managed at last.

"A problem?"

He sounded strange and she looked up, her pulse skipping at the heat in his eyes. "With the option."

"Oh." He seemed to have the same trouble focusing on the paper in his hand. "Er…no, well, yes…there could be. This gives the owner the right to terminate your lease after two years with one month's notice. That's unrealistic for a business. I'd ask for three months at least."

"Oh, I didn't think of that." She nodded vigorously. "Right. I'll do that. Thanks for the advice."

"You're welcome."

She sent him a nervous glance. He seemed to be waiting for something. Her heart wouldn't stop pounding, and she couldn't seem to think of anything to say next.

"You don't have to pay me right away."

She stared at him, uncertain if he was serious or not. "Oh, well, why don't you just send me a bill."

"I'd rather take it out on lunch."

"Lunch?"

"Lunch. You know, that meal that comes between breakfast and dinner?"

She pulled a face at him. "I know what you meant. I just don't think it would be a good idea."

His face grew wary. "Give me one good reason why not."

She could give him half a dozen. None that she could tell him, however. How could she tell him that the sight of him made her weak, and that the slightest touch could make her forget all the reasons she has to stay immune to his dynamic appeal? How could she explain that she could not trust her heart again, especially with him, because he made her feel so much more passion than Jason had ever managed to do? That her pain over losing Jason was nothing compared to the agony she would go through if she allowed herself to love this man, knowing that she could never hold him?

"People might talk," she said, only half joking.

"So let them. How about Randolphs, at noon?"

She shook her head, even though every nerve in her body screamed at her to accept. "I'm sorry, Brad, I'm kind of busy. I have to find an apartment, and buy supplies and furniture for the office—"

"You have to eat sometime. Don't tell me you're going to let the chance of a little gossip dictate your life for you. I thought you were made of sterner stuff, Annie."

"It's got nothing to do with gossip—" she broke off as the door swung open and Marie hurried in.

"I'm so sorry…" She stopped short at the sight of Brad. Apparently flustered, she added lamely, "Nice to see you, Brad."

"I thought I'd stop by and give Annie here some unsolicited advice," Brad said easily. "Can't have the Carlson Company taking advantage of our new resident."

Marie gave him a weak smile. "I'm sure the lease is in order."

"Well, there *is* just this one point." He took the contract over to her and showed her the paragraph in question.

Marie's face flushed, and she avoided looking him in the face as they discussed the option.

Anne watched them, barely listening to the conversation. She was too busy wondering if every woman who came in contact with Brad Irving had that same reaction whenever he got too close. The thought strengthened her determination to keep her distance from the irrepressible charmer who seemed destined to break the heart of every woman who had the misfortune to fall for that compelling magnetism.

"I'll have to make a phone call." Marie headed for the door. "I'll be back in a few minutes. We should be able to settle this then."

The door swung behind her, leaving Anne alone once more with the last man in the world she wanted to be with right then.

"So, how about that lunch?"

She made herself meet his gaze. "Brad, I appreciate the invitation, but I've told you, I'm really busy—"

"You owe me, Annie."

Taken aback, she stuttered when she answered him. "I told you…send me a bill."

"I don't mean for the advice." His gaze dropped to her mouth. "Or are you going to tell me you've forgotten what happened on that mountain?"

Floundering, she strove to justify her stand. "Of course not. It's just that…" She gestured helplessly with one hand. "Brad…I…"

"We have to talk. We can't just forget what happened."

She was drowning. If she didn't make one last effort, she would lose the battle. "I've already forgotten," she said quietly. "It's better that way."

He looked as if she'd slapped him. "I see."

"I'm sorry, Brad." She fought back the tears, determined he'd never know how she really felt.

"So am I." He stared at her for a long moment then, before she realized what was happening, he grabbed her arms and pulled her into his chest.

"Damn you, Annie, stop fighting me," he whispered harshly.

She started to protest, but he smothered her words with his mouth, claiming her lips and her soul. Her mind spun out of control, and she forgot all her doubts, all her fears, everything except the firm grasp of his hands on her arms, the hard lines of his body jammed against hers, and his searching, conquering mouth that set her entire body on fire.

He let her go so suddenly she almost fell. "I won't believe that night meant nothing to you," he muttered. "You're letting that damn family feud sway your judgment. For once in your life, think for yourself, Annie. Don't judge me by other people's opinions."

She was trembling so hard she could actually feel her knees shaking. Before she could answer him, however, Marie burst through the door.

"I've got the approval," she said, waving the contract in the air. "I guess we have a deal."

"Good." He gave Anne one last, smoldering glance, then strode to the door. "Congratulations, Annie. I hope your new business will be an outstanding success."

She was still thanking him when the door closed behind him.

Anxious now to be rid of Marie, who seemed inclined to talk now that they were alone, Anne finished signing the papers. She answered Marie's questions as best she could, and finally ushered her out the door, saying she had another appointment.

At last she was alone in her new office, so barren

without furniture, with plenty of time to sort out the chaotic thoughts chasing through her mind.

Had she been too quick to judge Brad, based on pure gossip with nothing to back it up? Was she allowing a lifetime prejudice against his family sway her judgment?

She wandered to the door and looked out onto the busy street. The leaden sky promised another snowstorm before the day was out. Even now snowflakes danced in the wind, chased into flurries as the cars swept by and destroyed their bid to cover the recently plowed pavement.

Her grandfather had a favorite saying. There's no smoke without a fire. But small-town gossip had a way of taking insignificant incidents and blowing them up into major events. Maybe she'd been too quick to condemn Brad, based on hearsay alone.

Her pulse quickened as she considered her options. What if she took him up on his challenge? What if she did have lunch with him? Dinner? Heat swamped her body as her mind took her on the inevitable path. What if she slept with him again? Made love with him in that wild, abandoned way that drowned her in a passion of need and urgency and intense emotions such as she'd never known before?

She could end up getting terribly hurt, she reminded herself. Was she willing to risk another broken heart for a few weeks of happiness? It was a tough decision.

Too tough to tackle now, when she had so much else to do, she decided. She would put her affairs in order first, then she would decide what she wanted to do about Brad.

* * *

Anne spent the next week outfitting her office and looking for an apartment, and eventually found exactly what she wanted, in a quiet dead-end street. A three-story house had been converted into three apartments, and the top one was vacant. The rent was more than she'd wanted to pay, but the view of the mountains made the extra expense more than worthwhile.

All her furniture had been put in storage when she left Denver, and she was looking forward to arranging it all in her new home.

When the moving van finally arrived, her mother helped her unpack, saying she needed something to do now that the girls had gone back to college.

They were in the living room, unpacking Anne's collection of miniature houses, when Carol Parker asked casually, "Are you feeling all right, Anne dear? You look awfully pale and tired."

Knowing how her mother worried about her children's health, Anne was reluctant to admit she hadn't felt up to par lately. Poor sleeping habits tended to have a bad effect after a while.

"I'm fine," she lied cheerfully. "Just been real busy getting everything together." She looked around the apartment, satisfied with the results of her efforts. "This does look nice, don't you think?"

Carol unwrapped a tiny model of a church and stood it on the middle shelf of Anne's curio. "Very nice, dear. You are eating right, aren't you? You know you can come and eat with us any time you want."

Anne laughed. "Stop worrying, Mom. I'm perfectly capable of taking care of myself."

"I know, dear, but when one gets busy, it's so easy to neglect what's important."

"I'm getting plenty of healthy nutrition," Anne assured her.

Carol reached for another carefully wrapped package in the large packing case. "There isn't anything worrying you, is there?"

Alerted by the careful tone in her mother's voice, Anne gave her a sharp look. "Like what?"

"Well, you know." Carol shrugged her shoulders. "You know how people talk around here. I was wondering if anyone had said anything about the nights you spent on the mountain with that man."

Anne pursed her lips. "What would they say? It's really none of their business."

"Of course not. I heartily agree." Carol finished unwrapping the lighthouse. "Still, people do tend to imagine all sorts of things. And you know what a dreadful reputation that man has earned for himself."

Anne sat down on the arm of her leather lounger. "If you're trying to ask me if anything happened while I was up in that cabin, then say so."

Carol glanced at her. "It's none of my business, dear. I just want you to be happy, that's all. I know you are still hurting from that mess with Jason, but I was kind of hoping that once you got home and got on with your own life, you'd feel much better."

Uneasily wondering if her mother had guessed the truth, Anne said firmly, "I am feeling better. I'm just tired, that's all."

Carol nodded. "Well, try to get some rest, Anne. You don't want to get run-down, you know. It's so easy to pick up one of these nasty viruses going around.''

''It's okay, Mom.'' Anne got up and put an arm around her mother's shoulders. ''I'll be just fine. You worry too much.''

She planted a light kiss on her mother's cheek, then turned back to the unpacking. There was just no way she could tell her mother the truth about what happened in the mountains. Her mother never kept anything from her father. And the truth would be enough to give her father a stroke.

It wasn't worth fighting her family for a man who could so easily break her heart. The best thing she could do for all of them was forget that night in a secluded cabin on a snowy New Year's Eve, and pretend it never happened.

Chapter 9

A week later Anne felt secure enough in her new surroundings to invite her mother over to the office. "We'll have lunch first," she told her mother when she called her that morning. "I have a few calls to make, but I think I should be through by noon."

Her mother sounded excited at the prospect, and Anne smiled as she laid down the phone. The outing would do them both good, she thought, as she reached for her organizer. She needed a break.

The last two weeks or so had been pretty hectic. Setting up an apartment and an office at the same time had taken more effort than she'd realized. The project had left her drained and strangely lethargic. For someone who was usually bounding with energy, the listless feeling was worrying.

Shaking off her vague fears, she dialed the phone number of her ex-partners in Denver, Malcolm and

Kyle Stewart. They still owed her the check from their settlement of the dissolved partnership. Now that she'd gone so deeply into debt furnishing the office, it was time to call in the money due to her.

Malcolm answered the phone, and didn't seem in the least pleased to hear from her. "I'm tied up with something right now," he said, when she greeted him. "Perhaps I can get back to you?"

"This won't take long," Anne said firmly. "I was just wondering when you planned to send me my settlement check. I'm running into some pretty heavy expenses right now, and I could use the money."

On the other end of the line Malcolm cleared his throat heavily. "Yes...er...I've been meaning to call you about that. You remember the Downsvale project?"

Anne frowned. Shortly before she'd withdrawn from the partnership the company had landed a lucrative deal to design a large office complex called the Downsvale project in a Denver suburb. "Of course I remember," she said cautiously.

"Well, when the owners found out you would not be working on it as planned, they withdrew the contract. They gave it to Solomon's instead."

"They can't do that. We had a contract."

"Your name was on that contract, Anne. Grady informed me that since we had broken the terms of the contract, naming you as lead designer, they were within their rights to cancel. My guess is that Solomon offered them a better deal and they found an excuse to switch."

"I don't believe it." Anne rubbed her forehead

with her fingers in an attempt to ward off the beginning of a headache. "Have you talked to a lawyer?"

"Yes, I have." There was a short pause, then Malcolm added quietly, "I'm sorry, Anne, but under the circumstances, we feel compelled to reduce the amount of your settlement figure. Your backing out of the Downsvale project cost this company a great deal of money. My brother and I agree that you should bear some of the loss."

Anne tightened her mouth. She refused to give in to the feeling of panic sweeping over her. She had invested heavily in office furniture and supplies, relying on the settlement money to cover most of her debts. Anything less would put a serious dent in her capital. It would be weeks, maybe months before she could expect to turn a profit. She couldn't afford to lose one penny of that settlement. "How much of a reduction are we talking about?"

"Well, Kyle and I talked it over with the accountants, and we agreed that a fifty percent reduction would be fair to all sides."

"Fifty percent!" Anne gripped the phone tighter. "Now wait a minute. I paid more than that to join the partnership three years ago, and I've certainly earned the rest over that time. You can't penalize me for one lost project. That money belongs to me. We agreed on it and signed on it."

"That was before we knew about the Downsvale deal. We believe you owe us half the settlement figure for backing out of the project. We're simply taking it out of the check, instead of recuperating that amount from you later. It will save us all time and money in the long run." The pause that followed was ominous.

"I don't think any of us want to go through a court case over this, do we?"

"Watch me," Anne said grimly. "You'll be hearing from my lawyer within the week." She slammed down the phone, and promptly burst into tears.

Several minutes later, she pulled herself together. This wasn't like her at all. What on earth was the matter with her? She should be calling a lawyer, instead of sitting there feeling sorry for herself.

She reached for the phone book, intending to call Mark Peterson, the family lawyer. She punched out the first two numbers, then paused, her finger poised in midair. Mark and her father were great friends. They played cards together every week, and had lunch at least a couple of times a month. Mark was bound to mention that she'd been to see him, even if ethics prevented him from telling her father the reason. Knowing her father, he'd badger her until she told him why she needed a lawyer.

The last thing Anne wanted was family interference in this. Her mother would worry herself sick, and her father would probably take it upon himself to personally confront her ex-partners. He meant well, but there would likely be all kinds of repercussions. She couldn't take the chance of that happening. She'd have to find another lawyer. Preferably one that her family didn't know socially.

She flipped open the Yellow Pages and ran her finger down the short list. Apart from Mark, there were only a few lawyers who dealt with her kind of problem. Most she'd never heard of. One she definitely knew. Brad Irving.

Anne closed the telephone book and laid her aching

head on her arms. She needed a good lawyer. In spite of everything else Brad had been accused of, she'd heard only positive comments about the success of his practice. She knew nothing about the other lawyers listed in the Yellow Pages. She knew Brad personally. While she might not be able to trust him with her heart, she felt quite sure she could trust him with her legal problems.

Could she possibly hire him without her family finding out? Was it worth the risk? Much as she loved her family, she couldn't stand them interfering in her affairs. It was the main reason she'd moved to Denver in the first place. Why hadn't she just stayed there, instead of running back home with her tail between her legs? She could have saved herself and everyone else a lot of grief.

To her dismay a tear rolled down her cheek again. Alarmed at her sudden tendency to cry, she sat up and made a determined effort to concentrate on the problem. A big part of her reluctance to hire Brad was her personal feelings toward him. She would have to guard against that, and keep everything on a business level.

What it amounted to was another choice. She could either hire her family's lawyer and risk interference from them, or she could hire Brad and risk her family's anger if they found out, or go with a complete unknown who may or may not be competent to handle the problem. Knowing the Stewart brothers, they would hire the best lawyer in Denver. She had to fight fire with fire.

With an unsteady hand, she reached for the phone. She dialed Brad's number, knowing full well that in spite of all her reasoning, subconsciously she had made up her mind to call him from the first moment she'd realized she needed a lawyer.

Maybe she was being the biggest fool on earth. Maybe, somewhere in the back of her mind, was the idea that this was some kind of test—that dealing with him on a business level would help her know the real Brad behind all the rumors and gossip.

Whatever the reason, there was now no doubt in her mind that she had never intended to call Mark, or the unknown lawyers. Her finger hovered over the last number for a second or two, then, with a feeling that she was stepping off a cloud into empty space, she pressed the final button.

The feeling of letdown when a female voice answered almost made her hang up. Forcing herself to speak naturally, she asked for Brad.

"He's on an appointment," his secretary informed her. "Would you like to leave your number? I'll have him call you back."

Anne reluctantly gave her the number, wishing now that she'd taken time to think things through.

Her impulsiveness was going to get her in real trouble one day, she told herself later, as she drove to her parents' house to pick up her mother. Her habit of making rash decisions had already cost her more than one heartache. One day she'd learn to think before she acted. Still, she couldn't help a little spasm of excitement at the thought of seeing Brad again.

In spite of her best efforts, he hadn't been far from her thoughts since the day he'd walked out of her empty office and wished her success. She'd been too busy to spend much time watching for him in town, but once or twice she'd found herself walking down Main Street, half expecting to see his tall figure striding toward her.

At first, every time the phone rang she'd felt a quiver of apprehension, wondering if he was calling her. Every time she answered to someone else's voice, she felt a little pang of disappointment. Eventually she'd stopped expecting him to call her.

She wondered what his reaction would be when he got her message. Maybe he'd given up on her and wouldn't call back. He would probably think she was calling him for personal reasons. A thrill of anticipation curled in her stomach. Maybe she was, but she couldn't let him know that. Not yet. Not until she had him figured out. And that would take time.

Her mother chattered endlessly throughout lunch, while Anne did her best to do justice to the quiche and salad she'd ordered. When she pushed it away half-eaten, her mother frowned at her. "What's the matter, Anne? Are you ill? You usually have such a good appetite."

Unwilling to admit she felt a little queasy, Anne made up an excuse. "I had a huge breakfast. I guess I'm just not all that hungry."

Carol Parker studied her daughter's face. "You don't usually eat a big breakfast. The most I've seen you eat is a slice of toast."

With a feeling she was only getting in deeper, Anne improvised. "I was with a prospective client."

"Who's the client? Anyone I know?"

"I make it a habit never to discuss my prospects until I have the deal signed."

"Not even with your mother? You know I would never tell anyone."

Anne smiled at her mother's injured expression. "Don't worry, Mom, the second I get an assignment you'll be the first to know. By the way, did I hear Dad saying that he's been contracted to build that fantastic new bowling alley near the diner?"

To Anne's relief, her mother launched into an account of her husband's latest contract, and the subject of her lack of appetite was dropped. Only half listening to her mother's chatter, she wondered if Brad had called while she was out of the office. She glanced at her watch, then decided he was probably at lunch and hadn't had time.

By the time the waitress brought the bill Anne was in a fever of impatience to be back in her office where she could answer the phone if he called. *If* he called. He *had* to call. Only now did she realize how much she wanted to see him again. The knowledge worried her. She was letting her emotions rule her head again. She should never have called him.

"Anne, dear, whatever are you thinking about? You have a scowl on your face fierce enough to frighten a mad bull."

Startled out of her thoughts, Anne reached for the bill. "Sorry. I was just trying to work out a schedule, that's all." She looked pointedly at her watch. "I'm sorry, Mom, I really do have to go. I've got a ton of things to do."

Her mother looked disappointed. "I thought you were going to show me the office."

She'd completely forgotten. Smoothing her face into a smile she said brightly, "Of course I'm going to show you the office. We should go now, though, so that I have time to show you everything.''

''We could make it another day if you're busy.''

''Today's just fine.'' She signed the bill and replaced her card in her purse. ''Let's go.''

All the way back to her office she rehearsed what she would say to him if he called while her mother was there. She had been so stupid to call him. She couldn't possibly hire him to solve her problem. Nothing but trouble could come of it. She'd just have to think up some excuse why she'd called.

The second she opened the door she saw the red light blinking on her phone, indicating that she had a message waiting. She made herself take time to listen to her mother's various comments, and did her best to quell her irritation when her mother's suggestions contradicted her own choice of accessories or the placement of her furniture.

At long last, just when her patience was in danger of disintegrating, her mother glanced at the clock and exclaimed, ''Goodness, is that the time? I have to be getting home. I promised Fiona I'd watch Katy for her. Fiona is that nice young woman who lives next door, remember?''

Anne nodded, already on her way to the door.

''Such a shame, having to bring up a child all by herself. Nice little girl, too. Sharp as a tac. Do you know...''

Anne followed her mother outside, barely listening to her chatter about her next-door neighbors.

On her way at last, Anne drove too fast up the street and had to make herself slow down until she reached the highway. She answered her mother's questions with one syllable answers, and had to reassure her all over again that she was feeling just fine.

"Do you have time to come in for a cup of coffee?" her mother asked, as she climbed out of the car in front of the house.

"Sorry, I have to get back." She hadn't even turned off the engine, seething with impatience now to get back and listen to the message.

"Well, call me. And thanks for the lunch, and the tour of your office."

Anne waved a farewell and pulled away from the curb, with one question on her mind—what excuse could she give Brad for calling him?

Arriving back at the office in record time, she let herself in, then sat down at her desk and stared at the phone. Now that she was able to listen to the message, she couldn't bring herself to do so. What if the message was from someone else? The Stewart's lawyer, for instance. That thought galvanized her into action. She snatched up the phone and dialed the number of her answering service.

The moment she heard Brad's deep voice, the shivers began, chasing up and down her back with every word he spoke.

"Rita said you called. I'll be here most of the afternoon if you want to call me back."

She put the phone down with an unsteady hand. It had been impossible to judge his reaction from his tone. He'd sounded professional, and somewhat distant. More and more she wished she'd never called him. She couldn't think of a single reason she could give for the call except for the real one.

While she was still trying to come up with something, the phone rang suddenly, jarring the silence. She jumped violently, and made a grab for the phone. In her haste she dropped the receiver with a loud clatter on the desk, and had to quickly scoop it up to her ear.

Her breathless greeting was answered immediately. "Anne? Are you okay?"

She closed her eyes and tried to regain her breath. "Yes, I'm fine, Brad. Thanks for calling back. I was just about to call you."

"I thought maybe something was wrong. I left a message for you to call back."

"Yes, I'm sorry…I took my mother to lunch and I've just taken her home."

"Ah, the three-martini lunch, I assume."

"Actually one small glass of wine, but who's counting."

"So, how's the ankle?"

"The ankle's fine, thanks."

"Good. Then what can I do for you?"

He'd already done more than enough to her composure, Anne thought frantically. "Oh, well, I ran into a little problem and I thought you might be able to help out, but on second thought, I think I can handle it myself."

She waited through the short pause, aware of her heart beginning to pound.

"You called me on an impulse, then instantly regretted it. Isn't that it?"

Her shoulders sagged. "Something like that."

"Why don't you tell me what the problem is, and then we'll decide if you can handle it alone."

Deciding that at this point, she really had nothing

to lose, she repeated the entire conversation she'd had with Malcolm Stewart that morning. Even as she reached the end of her story, she knew she needed help. Brad's help.

She wasn't at all surprised when he said brusquely, "You were right to call me. I can take care of this for you. Did you work at all on the project?"

"Just the preliminary sketches."

"Did you personally sign the contract for the Downsvale project?"

"No, I didn't. Malcolm handled the agreement and signed for the partnership."

"All right. Let me call them and I'll get back to you."

Her feeling of relief was almost overwhelming. "Thanks, Brad. I really appreciate this."

"You might not want to thank me when I tell you what my fee will be."

Her fingers tightened on the phone. "I'm sure it will be reasonable."

"Very reasonable. I want to take you to dinner."

She should have seen it coming, but she hadn't. Playing for time, she did her best to sound indifferent. "Shouldn't that be the other way around?"

"All right. You can take me to dinner." He paused, then added, "Unless you're afraid of what people might say."

She hesitated for the space of a heartbeat, then said quietly, "No, I'm not afraid of what people might say. What I do with my personal life is my own business. I'll be happy to take you to dinner."

The pleased surprise in his voice made her pulse

leap. "All right! Would you like me to make the arrangements, or would you prefer to do that yourself?"

"I'll do it. How about tomorrow night? Seven?"

"Sounds good to me." Again he hesitated. "I'd like to pick you up, but—"

"It's all right," she swiftly assured him. "I have my own apartment now." She gave him the address, then hung up. It would have to be Randolph's, she thought feverishly. But then everyone in town would know she was out with Brad. Including her family. That was something she would have to face.

She knew now that she'd embarked on this dangerous path because she wanted to give Brad a chance to prove himself. She had condemned him from the start, without giving him the benefit of the doubt. He deserved that at least.

As for her family, they would just have to understand that she couldn't be governed by a silly feud that should have been over long ago. No matter how they felt about it.

Long after she hung up on Brad, she continued to sit at her desk, her chin on her hands, going over the entire conversation with him again. That's what she admired most about him, his confident way of meeting a problem head-on and dealing with it. Nothing seemed to faze him, except that last time she'd seen him, when he'd marched out of her office with that bitter look on his face, wishing her success.

There was also the time when he'd looked her father in the eyes and told him that they were nothing more than ships that passed in the night. Had he really meant that, or had he just said those words to diffuse an ugly situation? Had he been protecting her? She wanted to believe that, so much. Maybe now, she'd find out. One way or the other.

She called Randolph's before she could change her mind, and made the reservations for the following night. Then she sat for several minutes after that trying to make up her mind if she should tell her mother first, or wait until she found out about it. Which wouldn't take long.

Deciding it was better not to make trouble before she had to, she did her best to forget about her upcoming date and worked on setting up her accounts system on the computer. By the end of the afternoon she felt exhausted, and put her weariness down to the emotional upheaval of the day.

It wasn't until later that evening that something else occurred to her. Something that she should have realized before this, and probably would have if she hadn't been so caught up with the ordeal of moving and setting up her office. Something that she'd thought about in the cabin, then promptly dismissed from her mind. Something that she knew could no longer be ignored.

Her period was at least two weeks overdue.

She sat in her living room, fighting a wave of panic so deep she could hardly breathe. There could be so many reasons why she was late. Maybe she was coming down with a cold. All the hassle of the last two weeks could have upset the timing. Maybe her quitting the Pill had something to do with it. Some women did miss one now and again without any good reason.

Some women might, but not her. Until now she'd always been as regular as the setting sun.

She couldn't be pregnant. It was too impossible to even think about. She got up from the chair and began pacing the room, picking up a cushion to plump it, moving a stack of catalogues to a different spot on the coffee table, anything to distract her mind from the very real possibility staring her in the face.

She could very well be pregnant. With Brad Irving's baby. If so, she was facing a catastrophe that would make her breakup with Jason seem nothing more than a frivolous misunderstanding.

Chapter 10

Anne's first instinct was to cancel the reservations at Randolph's. The last person in the world she wanted to be with right now was Brad Irving. If what she suspected was true, she would have to tell him the truth. She couldn't imagine what he would say. She didn't even want to think about it.

By the time she went to bed she'd convinced herself she was overreacting again. There was no point in risking an ulcer worrying about something that might never happen. If she canceled on Brad now, he'd think she was running scared because of her family, and she was determined to lay that particular theory to rest.

She chose a simple black dress to wear the next evening, and relieved the starkness of it with a thick gold chain and earrings. Her complexion seemed unusually pale, and she fluffed a generous dab of blush on her cheeks, then darkened her lashes with a touch of mascara. Exchanging her normal light lipstick with a brighter shade, she peered at her reflection in the mirror, trying to reassure herself that she looked her normal healthy self.

The ring of her doorbell shattered her nerves, and she dropped the uncapped lipstick in the sink, leaving a dark red stain smeared across the white porcelain. Quickly she cleaned off the mark, dried her hands, then with one last glance at the mirror, headed for the door.

Brad was leaning against the doorjamb when she opened it. He gave her a thorough up-and-down inspection that made her toes curl. "Nice." He peered past her into her living room. "Do we have time for the tour?"

"Sure." She stood back to let him in, then closed the door behind him. Taking a deep breath, she turned around to watch him walk through her living room.

He was wearing a dark gray suit. His pure white shirt and silver-blue tie tied everything together with just the right touch of casual elegance. He looked every inch the successful lawyer, supremely confident and in complete command of his world. Right then she would have given anything to shake that awesome composure and tell him she was pregnant with his child.

She couldn't just blurt it out like that, of course. For one thing, she couldn't be sure she was pregnant. If she was, she would have to think things through very carefully before giving him the bad news. There was no doubt in her mind that she would have to tell him. He at least deserved to hear it from her, and not from some whispering gossip behind his back.

She could just imagine his reaction. The experienced playboy, the romancer, the man so much in control of his destiny, foiled like a careless teenager from one night of passion.

Her bitterness unsettled her. It was as much her fault as his. She hadn't tried to stop what was happening. Just the opposite, she'd welcomed it with open arms. Literally. How could she blame him when she'd been such a willing and eager partner?

Miserably she watched him as he wandered around her living room. He sat down on her cream couch and patted the dark blue cushions, then rose again to inspect the contents of her curio.

"You're a collector," he said, as he studied the tiny miniature houses. "I wouldn't have imagined that. You don't seem the type."

"What type is that?"

He glanced at her over his shoulder. "Oh, I don't know. All that quiet efficiency and practical nature. People like that usually don't clutter up their lives with a lot of unnecessary junk."

"Are you suggesting that my expensive collection is junk?"

He grinned. "Of course not. Wrong word. A Parker would never have junk in the house."

She eyed him suspiciously, wondering if he was taking a stab at her family again. Deciding not to pursue it, she glanced at her watch. "We'll be late if we don't leave now."

"Oh, right." He glanced at the hallway leading to

her bedroom. "I'll have to take the rest of the tour later."

Not if she had anything to say about it, Anne thought grimly. Enough damage had been done already. Even so, the thought of him in her bedroom sent a thrill of excitement skimming down her back, and she had to force herself to think about something else before her mind led her where she definitely should not go.

Brad drove carefully through the streets of town, mindful of the slick roads and the woman at his side, for whose safety he was once more responsible. He'd received quite a jolt at the first sight of her tonight. He'd never seen her look more beautiful, or more desirable. He'd had a hard time controlling the urge to take her in his arms and crush her tantalizing mouth with his until she begged for mercy.

Being in her apartment had been unsettling. There was always something so intimate about a woman's apartment, as if she were exposing innermost secrets of her true self. Walking around Annie's apartment had made him feel privileged. It wasn't a word he would have used to describe the experience until now.

He tried to analyze why he should feel so differently about Annie's home, and couldn't come up with an answer. He only knew that she could make him feel vulnerable, in a way no woman had ever done before. It wasn't an entirely comfortable thought.

He watched her all through the meal, fascinated by the dimple that flashed in and out of her cheek when she smiled. He'd first noticed that dimple in the cabin, and the memory of that night still haunted him with a bittersweet hunger that wouldn't go away.

After many hours of arguing with himself in the long, predawn hours when he hadn't been able to sleep, he'd finally accepted the fact that Annie wasn't interested in a repeat performance. It had been a blow to his pride at first, but as the resentment faded he'd felt a deep sense of regret, knowing what he'd lost, and had never really had. He knew that he'd let something very special slip though his fingers, and was helpless to do anything about it.

He'd realized, that day in her office, that he didn't mean enough to her, that their night together hadn't meant enough to her, to risk alienating her family. In a way, he couldn't really blame her. It would be a lot to ask of any woman. But for Annie, who was so close to her parents, so loyal to her family, it was asking the impossible.

When he heard her message yesterday, asking him to call her, he'd been pleasantly surprised. He hadn't expected to hear from her again. When she'd agreed to meet him for dinner, he'd been astounded. Though he had no illusions about her motives. This was strictly a business deal. He'd be a fool to hope for anything more than that.

He roused himself from his depressing thoughts, aware that she had asked him a question he hadn't heard. "I'm sorry, I was thinking about something. What did you say?"

"I asked if you'd heard anything from the Stewarts."

"Not since yesterday. These things take time. I'll let you know as soon as I get a reaction from them."

"Thank you. I'd appreciate that."

"You're welcome. It gives me something to do. Things are usually pretty quiet this time of year. I get bored if I'm not busy with something."

Her beautiful green eyes seemed to gaze into his soul. "Are you planning on opening Coldwater again?"

The question took him by surprise. He took a moment to compose his thoughts before answering. "Not really. I've been too busy with other things."

"Are you ever going to open it again?"

"I don't think so."

"So what do you plan to do with the land?"

He was beginning to feel uncomfortable. He couldn't escape the idea that someone, perhaps her father, had briefed her on questions to ask him. "Why the avid interest?" he asked lightly.

"Oh, I don't know. I guess I just hate to see prime land sitting around unused." She studied him with frank curiosity. "If you don't have any plans for it, why don't you sell it?"

"Right. To the Parkers, I suppose."

The words were out of his mouth before he could stop them. He saw her flush and cursed himself for being so defensive.

"No, not necessarily to the Parkers," she said quietly. "I'm sorry. It's none of my business what you do with your property."

Ashamed of his unwarranted suspicions, he reached for his wineglass. "I can't sell the land. My father stipulated in his will that it was never to be sold. If it goes up for sale the local government can claim it and use it for whatever they see fit."

Her eyes widened. "Why would he do that?"

"Can't you guess?"

She stared at him for several seconds, understanding dawning in her eyes. "I don't believe it."

"Believe it." He drank some of the wine and set down the glass. "He was determined the land would never fall into Parker hands. Which is why he killed himself trying to hang on to it."

She shook her head in disbelief. "I can't understand why our families insist on maintaining this silly feud. It should have been over long ago."

"I couldn't agree more. If there was some way to end it I'd do it. Unfortunately anything I do only makes matters worse. I guess the Parkers and the Irvings are destined to be at each other's throats for generations to come."

To his surprise, she seemed upset by his words. Surely she knew as well as he did how firmly entrenched the families were in their opposing views. His own mother would rather dart into a stream of rush hour traffic than meet face-to-face with the Parkers.

If he didn't know better, he'd say that was guilt he saw lurking in Annie's expression, though he couldn't imagine why she would feel guilty. Maybe her father really had pressured her into finding out about the land. Somehow he couldn't see Annie complying with that.

"I think it's time I was getting home," she murmured, gazing at her watch. "I have an early call in the morning."

Concerned, he noticed she looked a little pale.

"Are you all right? Did I say something to upset you?"

She shook her head and sent him a fleeting smile. "Just tired, that's all. It's been tough getting everything taken care of, but things should be settling down now."

"I'm glad to hear it." He pushed his chair back and stood. "Don't worry about this little problem with your ex-partners. I'm sure we can get it straightened out without too much hassle."

"I'm sure you can." She rose from her chair, reaching for her purse behind her. "I have the utmost confidence in you."

Her comment gave him a rush of warmth. "Well, thank you, ma'am. I'll do my best to live up to your expectations."

Instead of laughing, as he expected, she gave him a long, searching look that left him wondering exactly what it was he'd said to provoke that intense scrutiny.

All the way home in the car Anne sat scrunched on her seat, wondering how in the world she was going to tell Brad if it turned out she was pregnant.

It would be traumatic under the best of circumstances. She couldn't even begin to imagine how her family would take it.

She wondered if he would offer to marry her. The thought brought a rush of longing so fierce she caught her breath. If only they'd been madly in love, planning to get married with the family's blessing, her news might have been easier to accept.

She couldn't marry him, of course. In the first place, she couldn't marry a man knowing he'd been forced into it out of a sense of duty. She couldn't bear that. He'd said it himself. *Being trapped in a situation like that is not my idea of a good life.*

In the second place, even if she were convinced he could love her, a marriage between an Irving and a Parker could very well set off World War III. That's if her announcement of her pregnancy didn't cause it first.

She almost groaned out loud. The suspense was just too much to bear. Tomorrow she'd take the damn test and find out for sure. No matter what happened, things were bound to get pretty gruesome. How complicated their lives had become. Things had been so much simpler when they were kids. She closed her eyes, remembering the lithe figure of her blond Viking striding across the schoolyard with her childish words echoing after him. *I hate you, Bradley Irving. I hate you.*

But she didn't hate him. She loved him. Her eyes flew open and she sat bolt upright. Dear God, *she loved him.* She always had. Ever since that first day when she'd landed at his feet in the schoolyard of Pike Elementary.

"Annie? Are you okay? Are you sick?"

Oh, God. Just when she thought things couldn't get more complicated, they just had. "No, I'm fine. Really." Her voice sounded weird, even to her.

Evidently Brad must have heard it, too. He laid a hand on her arm, making her jump violently. "Annie, tell me, what's wrong."

"Nothing!" She swallowed, and fought to regain her composure. He mustn't know. No matter what happened. No matter if she was pregnant or not. He must never know how she felt about him. "Just a little bit of indigestion." She managed a weak smile. "Guess I'm not used to all that rich food."

He continued to glance at her, his dark blue eyes narrowed against the lights of the oncoming cars. "I can pull over if you like."

This time she actually managed a laugh. "It's not that bad. I'll take some antacids when I get home and I'll be fine." In a desperate bid to change the subject, she asked him about his practice, though she paid scant attention to his answers.

Now that she'd finally admitted her true feelings to herself, the thought of possibly carrying his baby took on a whole new meaning. Whatever happened, she vowed silently, his child would grow up loved and cherished by every member of her family. She'd make sure of that.

Part of her, the major, sensible part of her, hoped that her suspicions were wrong, and that there was some simple explanation for her being overdue. Another part of her, the romantic, idealistic part of her longed to hold his baby in her arms. At least, she thought sadly, if they couldn't work things out, she'd have part of him forever in her life.

The car halted with a jerk, and Brad cut the engine. "Annie, stop lying to me. Something is wrong, isn't it. Is it something I said? Something I didn't say? Are you sick? What? Please tell me or I won't sleep tonight for worrying about you. And I know you don't want that on your conscience."

In spite of his light tone, she could hear the underlying anxiety, and she was truly touched by his concern. Turning to him, she gave him her warmest smile. "Brad, please, it's nothing. Just a slight head-ache and a touch of heartburn."

His gaze seemed to probe deep into her mind, until she was sure he could read her chaotic thoughts. "All right," he said finally. "But I'm going to call you tomorrow. Early. Just to make sure you're okay."

"Okay."

"Thanks for dinner."

She sighed. "You paid for dinner. You insisted, remember? I should be thanking you. And I will. Thank you for a lovely meal."

"I paid? How extremely generous of me." His grin reassured her. "Well, thanks for coming, anyway."

"My pleasure."

"Annie..." Her name slipped from his lips in a long sigh. He leaned forward, and she knew he was about to kiss her. Knew it with a sudden soaring of her heart and a rush of heat in her veins.

Nothing in the world could have stopped her from leaning into him, eager for his mouth on hers. Her mind reeled when he drew her closer, and she clung to him, helpless in the swirl of fire leaping between them. She wanted to drown in that kiss, forget all her troubles and think only of his mouth, his urgent tongue, and his hands roaming her quivering body.

He drew back, his voice a harsh whisper. "How about a nightcap? Can I come in?"

She was oh, so tempted. Common sense pounded in her brain, reminding her of everything she had to lose by loving this man. She needed time to think. She needed space. "I'm sorry, Brad. I'm really tired." Quickly she opened the door and scrambled out. "Drive carefully."

''Talk to you tomorrow.''

She couldn't see his face in the dark, but she could tell from his tone that he was disappointed. He drove away, and she watched his taillights turn the corner, the cold feeling already creeping around her heart. She loved him. She was very likely having his child. And there was no way in the world that she could marry him. Even if he asked. There was nothing she had ever seen or heard of sadder than that.

The sound of the phone ringing woke her up the next morning. The night had been long and restless. Her covers were in a tangle, her pillow was half off the bed, and the vague memories of a stressful dream still lingered in her mind.

She reached for the phone, and was jolted awake by the sound of Brad's voice. ''Did I wake you up?''

''No,'' she lied. ''I've been awake for some time.''

''You don't sound too chipper.''

Relieved by his normal, cheerful tone, she said lightly, ''I haven't had my usual shot of caffeine yet.''

''Ah, well that could account for it.''

The thought of coffee made her stomach heave. Hastily transferring her thoughts to cold, clear water, she said quickly, ''I'm sorry, Brad, but I have to run. Thanks again for dinner last night. I enjoyed it.''

''So did I. Let's do it again sometime.''

Her heart skipped a beat. His persistence was gratifying, and she had to remind herself of all the reasons she couldn't go out with him again. ''Sure.'' She hung up and made a mad dash for the bathroom.

Later that day he called her again at the office. Her initial thrill of pleasure at the sound of his voice could not be suppressed, no matter how much she tried.

"I've had a long talk with the Stewart's lawyer," Brad said, after asking if she was feeling better. "They want to meet with us. Looks as if we'll have to take a trip to Denver."

Her pulse leapt. "Can't they come here?"

"They could, but since they requested the meeting, it's probably in our best interests to go to them."

A trip to Denver was the last thing on her list of things she wanted to do. Especially in the company of Brad Irving. "Can't you handle it without me?"

"Sorry. Mason's insisting we both go."

"All right, if it's unavoidable, I guess I'll go."

"I'll pick you up first thing in the morning."

"No!" The way her stomach was behaving lately, she needed at least a couple of hours to settle it down. "I...have an appointment first thing. Can we make it around ten?"

"We could. That will cut it a little fine. Can't you postpone your appointment?"

"Not without a hassle."

"I could get the Stewarts to postpone, but Mason has a pretty tight schedule. It could be a while before we get another appointment."

"No," she said quickly, "I'd like to get this over with as soon as possible."

"All right. I'll be at your apartment at ten sharp."

"I'll be ready." She paused. "And...thanks, Brad. I appreciate it."

"Are you quite sure you're feeling all right?"

"Quite sure." She hung up, and rested her forehead on her arms. All these lies and evasions were beginning to get her down.

Although she didn't want to admit it, somewhere

deep in her mind lay the certainty that once she broke
the news that she was pregnant with Brad's child, she
would never be alone with him again. Even if she
opposed her family. She willingly would do that if
she could have been certain Brad loved her. There
was no way she could ever be sure of that. And she
could never settle for less.

On the way home from the office she bought the
pregnancy test kit. Standing in her kitchen that evening, she waited with one eye on the clock for the
prescribed time to elapse.

When it was time to check out the test tube, she
found it impossible to move, and found all kinds of
things to do to avoid going back in that bathroom.

Finally she could put it off no longer. Steeling herself, she opened the bathroom door and approached
the sink where she'd left the tube. One look confirmed
her worst fears. She was pregnant. With Brad's child.

Although she had more or less expected it, staring
right at the evidence made it all frighteningly clear.
She had committed the unpardonable sin. Not only as
far as her family was concerned, but Brad as well.
She had slept with her family's bitter enemy, and she
was bearing his child.

That night Anne's mother called her, and she knew
immediately by the guarded voice on the phone that
someone had spotted her with Brad at Randolph's.
Apparently whomever it was had wasted no time in
relaying the news.

"Anne, dear," her mother said carefully, "I heard
something rather strange today. Jessie swears she saw
you with Bradley Irving in Randolph's last night. I

told her that couldn't possibly be true, of course. I mean, what would you, of all people, be doing with a man like that?''

Anne drew a deep breath. "It is true, Mom. I was with Brad last night. It was a business dinner. He's handling a legal matter for me.''

Her mother's shocked gasp echoed down the line. "Anne Beatrice Parker! Are you telling me you actually hired that man? What's the matter with Mark, may I ask? Has he suddenly developed some contagious disease that I haven't heard about?''

Anne closed her eyes. "There's nothing wrong with Mark as far as I know," she said wearily. "This is a very delicate matter, and I just felt that Brad was more qualified to handle it. He is a corporate lawyer, after all.''

"Mark has handled all your father's concerns since before you were born. And handled them beautifully, I might add.''

Including her father's attempts to wrest a parcel of land away from its rightful owners, Anne thought stubbornly. "I know that, Mother, but Mark's methods are old-fashioned and outdated. I felt in this case I needed someone who was more in tune with the modern concepts of legal rights. There is a lot of money riding on this, and frankly, I can't afford to lose.''

"What money? What are you talking about?''

Briefly Anne explained, wishing she didn't have to go into the matter with her mother.

"Why didn't you discuss this with us first?" her mother demanded when she was finished. "I'm quite sure Mark could have handled it. I don't know what your father is going to say when he finds out. He's likely to have a stroke, you know."

Anne compressed her lips. "Does he have to know?"

"Well, of course he has to know. If I don't tell him, someone else will. Really, Anne, I can't believe you are being so irresponsible. Living in Denver certainly hasn't done you much good."

"I'm sorry, Mother, but it's done now. Brad is handling this matter for me and I'm sorry if that upsets you and Daddy, but I had to protect my interests in this case."

"And who is going to protect your father's interests, might I ask?"

"I'm sure you can handle Daddy," Anne said smoothly. "After all, you've been doing it all my life."

She hung up finally, feeling as if she were setting herself adrift on an endless ocean with no land in sight. No matter which way she turned, there was a big, fat chasm just waiting for her to fall into it. She had never felt quite so alone in her entire life.

She slept little that night, and when she finally crawled out of bed the next morning, her stomach revolted and she had to make a wild dash for the bathroom. Emerging a few minutes later, she made her decision. She would tell her parents first. Then she would find a way to face Brad with the news. But not yet. First she had to get this matter with the Stewarts settled. She would need the money more than ever now.

Besides, she needed time. Time to rehearse how she would give the news to her parents. And time to find the words that would send Brad out of her life forever.

Chapter 11

When Brad arrived that morning, Anne was ready and waiting for him.

She'd chosen a simple light gray pantsuit to wear to the city, and her new black boots. She'd brightened the outfit with a cherry-red sweater, and carried her navy blue wool coat out to the car.

The recent snowstorms had left huge piles of muddy-looking snow at the sides of the road, thrown there by the snowplows. The sun shone sporadically through the gray clouds as they headed out on the highway, and Brad was able to make good time.

He turned on the radio to a popular music station, and they passed the time in a lively discussion of the latest music styles and artists. Although on the surface, their exchanges were lighthearted, Anne was aware of a subtle tension between them that had probably been generated by her obvious reluctance to let him come into her apartment last night.

She sent him a swift glance, trying to gauge his mood. It was hard to tell with Brad. He had a way of covering up his true feelings behind that relentless sense of humor that never seemed to desert him.

He wore a dark blue shirt with his black suit, and a bright, multicolored tie that somehow made him look sophisticated and terribly modern. Again she was struck by the contrast to the man she'd made passionate love with in the cabin. It was almost as if he were someone else.

There was still so much she didn't know about him.

If only she knew how he really felt about her. If only she could believe he meant the wonderful things he'd said to her. How many times had he said the same things to somebody else? How could she believe him, knowing what people in town said about him? What he'd told her himself about his attitude toward relationships? *I believe in variety. Does that make me a bad person?* No, she thought miserably. Not a bad person. Just a man she couldn't trust with her heart.

The song on the radio came to an end, and the announcer welcomed everyone to the station. Anne was only half listening to him, until he said something that startled her out of her uneasy thoughts.

"The storm should hit the Denver area by two this afternoon," the voice announced. "This is a big one, folks. Better get dug in for the long haul. At least a foot, maybe more. Road crews are standing by to maintain the major freeways, but side roads and outlying areas could prove to be a problem for the next day or two. Catch the whole story at the station break at twelve.''

"Oh, great," Brad muttered by her side. "That should make it fun on the road back. Great timing."

Anne stared at him in dismay. "The meeting's at one. We'll have to get out of there before it hits."

"We can try." He sent her a wry glance. "But if it's coming in from the west as it usually does, these roads will be covered long before it hits Denver. Look back there."

He nodded at his rearview mirror, and Anne craned her neck to see out the rear window. Sure enough, a ridge of thick clouds had loomed up behind them, looking like a wall of dense black smoke against the metal-gray sky. Brad was right. The storm was coming in fast. She might very well be stranded in Denver with him.

Heat spread rapidly though her veins. This wasn't the mountain and a snowbound cabin, she reminded herself fiercely. This was a city, with separate hotel rooms. Separate hotels if need be. "Maybe we should turn back now," she murmured, knowing how futile that would be.

"We're almost there now. Do you really want to turn back? We'll probably run into it, anyway."

"I guess not. I really would like to get this matter over with."

"Then I say we take our chances with the storm."

"All right." She tried to relax. Brad knew what he was doing. They'd make it back all right.

Brad made her eat lunch before heading into the office complex where the Stewarts were waiting for them with their lawyer.

Malcolm greeted Anne with his usual buoyant comments and shook Brad's hand with exaggerated enthusiasm. His brother, Kyle, seemed ill at ease, and couldn't quite meet Anne's eyes when she spoke to him.

John Mason, the Stewart's lawyer, was a serious-looking man with thick black-rimmed spectacles no doubt chosen to give him a look of authority. Anne had met him only a couple of times during her association with the Stewarts, and she hadn't been particularly impressed.

Mason was inclined to bluster, using unconventional terms that were difficult to understand in the hopes of confusing his adversaries. Not at all like Brad, who remained calm and reasonable, in spite of Mason's attempts to rattle him.

"Mr. Stewart," Brad began, after listening patiently to Mason ramble on about the company's position on the disputed settlement. "How much profit has this company made in the past three years?"

"I have the figures here," Mason said, "But—"

"Excuse me, Mr. Mason. I believe I directed that question at Mr. Stewart."

"Of course we made a profit," Malcolm Stewart said, beginning to lose his affable expression. "That's no secret. We wouldn't be in business if we didn't."

"I fail to see what the last three years has to do with anything," Mason protested, but Brad ignored him.

"And during that period, Ms. Parker produced satisfactory work?"

"Very satisfactory. But—"

"And when she signed the agreement to join the

partnership three years ago, she contributed fair compensation for her share of the company?''

"Well, yes, but—''

"Then you would say that she lived up to the terms of that agreement until the day she resigned from the company?''

"It was when she resigned that the trouble began,'' Kyle put in, giving his brother a warning glare.

Anne glanced at Brad, impressed by the expert way he was handling the situation. He was the only one at the table who seemed perfectly at ease and supremely confident. She tried to imagine Mark Peterson handling the exchange with as much assurance and proficiency, and failed. She had made the right choice. And if she could have picked any man to be the father of her child, she would still have chosen Brad Irving. Even though she would have to bring up his child by herself.

She wasn't really surprised when, in the face of a lawsuit, the Stewarts backed down and agreed to pay her the entire settlement figure.

Kyle's expression was thunderous as they rose from the table, but Malcolm shook her hand and wished her luck with her new business.

Brad thanked John Mason, then ushered Anne out of the office with a firm hand on her arm. She waited until they were out of the elevator before saying, "Thank you, Brad. I'm truly grateful. Please, send me a bill. I'll feel better if I can pay you.''

He sent her a sidelong glance as they crossed the polished floor of the lobby. "You don't have to feel obligated. I did it as a favor. In return for your efforts in the cabin.''

Speechless, she could only glare at him. "I beg your pardon?"

He halted, grinning at her. "Climb down from that pedestal of outrage. I meant your cooking and cleaning efforts."

"Oh." Now she felt foolish.

"Not that I didn't enjoy the rest of it. Because I did. Very much."

She felt as if all the breath had rushed out of her lungs. "I think it's time we left." She started for the door but he reached out for her arm again.

"Annie. I'm sorry if I'm embarrassing you. I'm sorry if you find this entire subject uncomfortable. I just want you to know that I thought that what happened between us on that mountain was beautiful, incredible and unforgettable. I don't want you to think that it meant nothing more to me than a fun way to relieve the boredom."

"I don't. I—" She shut her mouth before she blabbed out the truth. That every moment she was with him was both joy and pain, a bittersweet memory to hold in her heart in the empty years ahead. No matter how she tried, she couldn't forget what he'd told her that day in the cabin. Why did she have to fall in love with a man who thought of marriage as a prison, and meaningful relationships as a trap?

"It's getting late." She pulled her arm from his grasp and hurried toward the revolving doors. She almost collided with the woman who emerged from the glass compartment, and saw with a shock the snowflakes clinging to her thick scarf. One glance outside told her the story. The storm had arrived.

Standing outside on the sidewalk, she shivered as

the wind drove the stinging snow in her face. Already the swirling white cloud drifted across the road, stirred up by the relentless tires of the passing cars. She pulled on her coat, grateful for its warmth.

"We could try to make a run for it," Brad said at her side. "But my guess would be that we wouldn't get very far. I suggest finding a hotel for the night and give the plows a chance to do their work. I really don't think we want to be stranded out there in the dark. I think we've both had more than enough of that."

He was buttoning up his raincoat as he spoke and she couldn't see his expression. Much as she hated to admit it, he was right. Trying to stem the feeling of panic, she asked unsteadily, "Where do you suggest?"

"The Preston is right around the corner. It's a fairly comfortable hotel, and has a great restaurant."

"I know. Henneker's. I've been there." It was in that restaurant that Jason had proposed to her. She couldn't imagine how she could have been so devastated by Jason's betrayal. It was obvious to her now that he was so wrong for her. And Brad was so right. She almost laughed at the irony.

The hotel had plenty of vacancies, and they had no trouble booking two rooms on the top floor. This time Anne insisted using her credit card, saying she refused to stay there if Brad gave her an argument.

Obviously reluctant to accept, he finally agreed. "I'll have to go shop," she told him, as they moved away from the counter. "Stuff like toothpaste and a toothbrush."

"Good idea. What about underwear?"

She glanced up at him, braced for one of his suggestive comments. "What about it?"

"Well, I don't know about you, but after our experience in the mountains I'm not too excited about wearing mine two days in a row again. I'd like to buy some spares."

She felt awkward discussing the subject with him. There was an intimacy about it that made her feel as if she were engaging in some kind of illicit rendez-vous with him. Which was nonsense, of course. "Well, I was planning on laundering mine in the bathroom sink, but if you want to shop for more I'll go with you."

"And help me pick them out?"

"I don't think so." She pulled a face at him. "I meant I'll shop, too. I'm always happy to have an excuse to go shopping in a department store."

"Then what are we waiting for?" He took her arm in that proprietary gesture that seemed to have become a habit with him. When they separated in the store to find their respective departments, Anne felt a sense of relief, as if she could finally let go of some of the tension she'd been under ever since they'd left Grand Springs that morning.

She had to pass through the infant section to reach the lingerie, and couldn't resist pausing at the racks of tiny garments. Aware that she was being premature, she subdued the urge to wander through the displays and hurried on to find what she needed.

She justified picking up the flimsy gold nightie and the pale blue sweater by assuring herself she could always use an extra. She paid for her purchases, then headed out into the jewelry department where she'd arranged to meet Brad.

She was admiring a diamond-and-sapphire necklace when she heard Brad's voice behind her. "All set?"

As always, the sound of his voice seemed to tingle all the way down her back. He'd always been able to affect her that way, she realized. Even when they were kids in grade school.

She smiled up at him. "You'd better get me out of here before I spend all that settlement you worked so hard to get for me."

"What is it about women that they can't walk into a department store without coming out loaded with stuff they don't need?"

She laughed at his comical expression. "Easy. They convince themselves they simply can't live without everything they see."

"That would certainly describe my mother."

She saw a flash of bitterness cross his face, and changed the subject. "It's too early for dinner. Would you be interested in taking a walk around the art museum? They have an exhibit of sixteenth-century architecture I'd really like to see."

She hadn't really expected him to show much interest for what had to be for him a dry subject, but he surprised her with his eager response.

"Great idea! I'd love that. I haven't visited the museum since they finished the renovations."

"Then you're in for a treat. The improvements are really extensive. They've opened up the sixth floor and put in a gallery for American and European art, and redesigned most of the other floors. There's so much more space there now. You'll love it."

"In that case, let's drop off this stuff and head right out."

Delighted that he shared her enthusiasm for the museum, she felt more animated than she had in days as she walked with him down the parkway toward the impressive building that housed so many magnificent treasures.

The walls of the museum soared in a gleaming mass of glittering tiles against the steel-gray sky. Snowflakes tumbled and swirled around it, reminding Anne of a medieval castle inside a snow globe. She had always loved this view, but today it seemed especially ethereal.

Once inside, the warmth seemed oppressive after the chilling snow-swept streets. She slipped out of her coat, and waited for Brad to do the same.

"Okay, lead on," he said, as he folded his raincoat over his arm. "You're the guide."

The exhibit was as extensive as she'd hoped, and even Brad seemed impressed by the variety of the architectural designs. She answered his questions as best she could, impressed by his knowledge of such a specialized subject.

Together they explored the seventh floor, devoted to art of the American West, a favorite for both of them. Brad admitted to being a huge fan of the Russell paintings and Remington sculptures. "I think I was a cowboy in another life," he told Anne, as they stood side by side admiring a bronze sculpture of a wrangler astride a rearing horse.

She studied him for a moment, then shook her

head. "I'm sorry, but you don't have the legs for it. They're supposed to be bowed."

"Like this?" He hobbled away from her, his knees pulled apart and his spine bent. He looked so ridiculous she had to laugh.

"That just looks like a bad imitation of the Hunchback of Notre Dame."

He came back to her, his gaze warm on her face. "I love to hear you laugh. It gives me such a good feeling inside. The kind of feeling you get when you're really cold and you step into somewhere warm and cozy."

Something deep inside her trembled. When he looked at her like that, spoke to her like that, it was all too easy to forget her fears and her doubts. A sudden longing to touch him was so strong, so intense, she stopped breathing.

The sound of the murmuring voices around them seemed to fade away as she stared into his dark blue eyes. The message in them couldn't be more obvious. Right then she knew he wanted her. And oh, how she wanted him.

Somehow she found her voice, and the strength to say lightly, "Well, if it's laughter you want, I have just the place to show you."

A fleeting expression of disappointment crossed his face, then he smiled. "Lead on, my fair one. I will follow you anywhere."

Simple words, spoken in jest. But how she wished they were true.

She led him down to the fifth floor, to the Discovery Library, which had been designed to look like part of an English country estate. After inspecting the exploration boxes and the CD-ROM stations, she led him to the costume closet which housed period costumes and wigs.

There she made him try on a magnificent seventeenth-century jacket, complete with ruffles and frills, and a powdered wig to go with it. When he perched a massive, wide-brimmed hat on his head, allowing the ostrich feathers to fall over one eye, she laughed so hard she collapsed against him.

He caught her, laughing with her, and for a few wonderful, magical moments she felt they were totally in tune, as if they had shared the joy of laughter for a lifetime.

Together they took off his costume jacket and hung the clothes back in the closet. As they walked away he caught hold of her hand, and it seemed so natural to leave it clasped in his as they wandered among the rest of the exhibits, exclaiming and pointing out interesting details.

Gradually the harsh realities of the world outside faded into oblivion. The hushed rooms felt cozy, and cloaked in an aura of fantasy. The strong grasp of his warm fingers gave her a sense of security, as if she'd finally found an anchor in that empty ocean. She wanted this day, this time, to go on forever, for right now, right this moment, they were truly together and nothing could ever take away the precious memory.

By the time they left the museum, the snow lay thick on the sidewalk, and the traffic had slowed almost to a stop. They made their way slowly back to the hotel, with the glittering lights of the city showing them the way.

When Anne slipped, Brad caught her by the elbow, then put his arm around her waist to hold her steady. Slithering and trudging through the snow together, they passed deserted coffee shops and empty stores. Farther on, from the fogged windows of a gaily lit bar, they heard the strains of a jazz band drifting on the cold night air. The plaintive sound of the horn echoed down the street, as if urging the passersby to hurry into shelter from the chill of the night.

Just before they reached the hotel he paused, and turned her to face him. Before she could register his intention, he lowered his head and covered her mouth gently with his. When she eagerly returned the pressure he caught her closer, wrapping both arms around her to draw her into his hard body. Oblivious and uncaring of the people scurrying past, she gave herself up to the sheer joy of the embrace.

She forgot everything that had gone before. There was only now, this moment, this snowy night on the streets of Denver, and Brad. Her heart seemed to swell with her love for him.

"I've been wanting to do that all afternoon," he told her, in a husky whisper.

She smiled. "So have I."

He kissed her again, just a mere brush of her lips with his, but there was such breathless promise in the gesture that thrills of anticipation chased through her veins. He caught her hand again, and together they entered the bright warmth of the hotel lobby.

She stood close to him in the elevator, her hand tucked with his in the pocket of his raincoat. An elderly woman smiled at her, and she wondered if the glow showed in her face. When they reached the top floor, she led the way out into the corridor with a sense of floating like a dandelion seed on the breeze.

"How long will it take you to get ready for dinner?" Brad asked, glancing at his watch. "It's almost five-thirty. I thought we might have a quiet drink in the lounge before going in to eat."

She smiled, feeling as if that slight movement of her face muscles was reverberating all over her body. "Give me about an hour?"

He heaved a wildly exaggerated sigh. "You're going to make me wait that long? How will I survive without you? How come it takes a woman so long to comb her hair?"

"Actually I was planning on a hot shower."

"Really? Mind if I join you?"

She gave him a playful shove. "Yes, I do mind. Go get your own hot shower."

He grasped her chin with his strong fingers and placed a firm kiss on her lips. "The way I feel now," he said softly, "I think I need a cold shower."

"Then you'd better go do it, before we both starve to death."

"So much for romance. Okay, an hour it is. Your place or mine?"

She grinned. "I'll come to your room and get you when I'm ready."

"I'll be waiting, princess."

She left him, still smiling, and let herself into her empty room. Eager not to waste a single moment more than she had to, she showered in a hurry. She felt like a kid again, getting ready for the high school prom. How well she remembered it—all the excitement, the breathless anticipation, and that wonderful, terrifying feeling that something really momentous could happen any moment to change her life forever.

If a little voice warned her that she was thinking dangerously, she ignored it. Tonight was hers, and tomorrow was a billion years away.

She wore the new blue sweater with her gray pants, and pulled her hair back into a more sophisticated style, fastening it with the glittering butterfly comb she'd bought in the jewelry department that afternoon. The sweater dipped low in front, and she wished now she'd bought a necklace to break up the expanse of bare skin.

She applied a light dusting of makeup, paying attention to her eyes. A faint smudge of blush was enough to complement the glow in her cheeks, and finally satisfied with the results, she let herself out of her room.

The corridor was deserted, and she could almost hear the pounding of her heart as she paused in front of Brad's door. Taking a steadying breath, she raised her hand and tapped on the door. This was their night, she thought, as she waited for him to answer her summons. Quite possibly the last night she'd spend with him. And she intended to make the most of it.

Chapter 12

The door opened almost immediately. Surprised, she noticed Brad wore a completely different outfit, and wondered if he'd shopped just for her benefit. The unbuttoned collar of his shirt revealed the strong line of his throat. He'd showered and shaved, and she could smell the faint fragrance of a sultry cologne, just enough to get her attention. He looked a little more like the unpretentious man in the cabin, and infinitely appealing.

He stood back to let her in and she entered warily, feeling suddenly nervous, though she couldn't have said why. He closed the door, then turned to study her in that intense way that always gave her shivers.

"Wow," he said softly. "I'd say the hour was worth every second."

Her smile felt weak. Her knees felt weak. Everything about her felt weak. "Thanks," she said unsteadily. "I could say the same for you."

His gaze locked on hers, freezing time. "We'd better get out of here," he said at last. "Before I forget I'm a gentleman."

He reached for his jacket and shrugged it on. "Tie?"

"Not if you don't want to."

"Good. Let's go then. I don't know about you, but I'm starved."

She was, too, she discovered, when the attentive waiter laid a plate of steaming soup in front of her. "Good," she announced, when she finally laid down her spoon. She looked up to see Brad grinning at her.

"I always did like to see a woman enjoy her food."

"Then you should have a good time tonight. All that walking this afternoon has given me an appetite."

"You're going to need it judging by the size of the steak you ordered. However did you manage to survive those skimpy meals in the cabin?"

"The same way you did. When it's all you've got, you make the most of it."

He laughed. "Good philosophy. I'll have to add that to my words-to-live-by list."

She studied him with interest. "What other words are on the list?"

"Oh, you know, the usual stuff. Look before you leap, don't burn all your bridges, don't borrow trouble."

"Ah, you're the cautious type. I should have known."

He gave her a quizzical look. "What's that supposed to mean?"

"It means you don't like to take risks."

"I do too take risks. I climb mountains, ski slopes, swim in lakes, drive too fast. I've even tried bungee jumping, though to tell you the truth, I wasn't too enamored with hanging upside down. All that blood rushing to my head at once was just a tad disorienting."

"Those are all physical risks. I meant emotional."

"Ah." He nodded. "I've been accused of that now and then, yes."

"Everyone has their Achilles' heel."

"So what's yours?"

She had to think about it. "Worrying too much. Caring too much about what other people think."

"People—as in your family?"

"And yours."

His mouth twisted in a wry smile. "Well, none of them are likely to know we are in Denver together. Not unless you tell them."

"I have no intention of telling them." This would be her secret, she promised herself. No one was going to spoil the memory of this night with ugly accusations and reprimands. No one.

Anxious to change the subject, she asked him what he thought of the renovations to the art museum, and they spent the rest of the meal discussing the various exhibits and exchanging views on European and American artists.

Brad was well-informed on the subject, and Anne thoroughly enjoyed their animated conversation. When the bill arrived she made a half-hearted attempt to use her own credit card, but Brad was adamant in his refusal to let her pay.

She led the way out of the restaurant, feeling an ache of sadness that the night was over. When they reached the top floor of the hotel, however, Brad slipped his hand under her arm. "Before you go back to your room, come to mine. I have something to give you."

Unsettled, she asked lightly, "Your bill?"

"No, not my bill. Quit worrying about that." He paused in front of his door and slid the card into the slot. "You were absolutely right, you know. You do worry too much about the wrong things."

"There are right things to worry about?"

"Definitely." He ushered her inside the room and closed the door. "World hunger, the environment, global warming, the economy, the threat of biological warfare, I can think of any number of things to worry about."

The fluttering in her stomach intensified as she watched him slide out of his jacket and toss it on the bed. Being enclosed in a hotel room with him was definitely on her list of things to worry about, she thought uneasily.

He sat down on the bed and pulled open the drawer of the bedside table. Mystified, she watched him take out a package and offer it to her.

She took it, and sat down on the bed next to him. Annoyed at the way her hand trembled, she fumbled with the distinctive wrapping from the department store they'd visited that afternoon. "What's the occasion? It isn't my birthday or anything and Christmas was a whole month ago."

"Just a little something to celebrate our victory."

"I should be buying you gifts for helping me—" She broke off with a gasp. The box inside looked familiar. Lifting the lid, she peeked inside, then carefully drew out the miniature house—the latest edition of her collection. "Brad, it's lovely! Wherever did you find this? I didn't even know it had been released yet."

"I happened to see it this afternoon when we were shopping for underwear and since I didn't remember seeing that one in your collection I took a chance and bought it."

She turned the tiny model of a Georgian mansion in her fingers, admiring the delicate, graceful lines, the exquisite ornate windows and steep roof that were so characteristic of that era. "You know, I've always wanted to design a real house just like this," she said softly. "Thank you."

She was afraid to look up, in case he saw her threatening tears. He couldn't have given her anything that would have delighted her more. His thoughtfulness surprised and touched her.

"I'm glad you like it."

"Oh, I do. But I can't help feeling that it should be the other way around. I owe you so much for everything you did. And here I am costing you money."

"There you go, worrying again." He laid his finger against her lips. "What did I tell you about that?"

His light touch sizzled on her mouth, and she caught her breath. Once more his intent gaze locked on hers. Then, as if by some mutual signal, she leaned toward him as his hot mouth replaced his finger.

Somewhere in the back of her mind she'd known

this was going to happen, and she'd welcomed it. She knew now that she would have been bitterly disappointed if he'd allowed her to go back to her room without attempting to make love to her.

He stood, and took the miniature house from her nerveless fingers, placing it on the bedside table before pulling her to her feet. "I haven't been able to take my eyes off you all evening," he murmured.

It seemed so natural to raise her arms and wind them around his neck. "Then what are you going to do about it?"

She saw his eyebrows rise, and knew he hadn't expected her to respond so eagerly.

"I know what I'd like to do about it."

Tilting her head back, she smiled up at him. "Tell me."

His gaze moved down to her mouth, robbing her of her breath. "I'd rather show you."

She felt wicked, reckless and unbelievably sure of herself. Somewhere in her mind a voice urged her to consider what she was doing. Being with him now could only bring her more pain. She ignored the warning. It was too late now. She wanted him. One last time. She went up on her toes and kissed him. "Then show me."

Flames leapt in his eyes, and his hands slid under her sweater. "My pleasure, ma'am," he muttered, then his mouth was on hers, fire meeting fire, obliterating all the doubts from her mind.

It was even better than the first time. Locked in his arms, her moist body writhing under his, she gave everything she had. Her mind blocked out everything except the man claiming her body and soul, while she strove to imprint every precious second in her memory. This was as love should be—no holding back, no inhibitions, no regrets. Even if this man could not love her the way she wanted him to, he had given her memories that would never die—memories that would sustain her and inspire her in the lonely years ahead.

Long after he'd fallen into a deep sleep at her side, she lay awake, committing forever to memory the feel of his naked body, the soft breath on her cheek, the weight of his arm across her belly. Knowing that his seed was growing inside her, she prayed she would have the strength to deny him if he offered to marry her. She knew, without a single doubt, that she would rather keep the memories of this incredible night frozen in her mind, than watch what they'd once had wither and die as he struggled to live the life he dreaded—trapped into a marriage he hadn't wanted.

She slept at last, and woke with a feeling of impending disaster. Though she did her best to return Brad's bantering comments, her heart wasn't in it. He ordered room service, and laughed at her when she hid in the bathroom to avoid facing the waiter. She didn't tell him that her nausea had forced her in there.

She made herself eat the Danish she'd asked for, and even managed a laugh or two when Brad told her about some of his weird cases. The intimacy of their shared breakfast was almost too much to bear, and when he finally suggested they head for home, she was more than ready to agree.

He kissed her once, long and hard, just before she went back to her room to shower. She fled from him with tears in her eyes and an almost unbearable ache in her heart.

The main highway back to Grand Springs had been plowed the night before, though once they turned north onto Highway 93, the road became much more difficult to navigate. Brad had to use his full concentration on the road, and Anne was glad of the excuse not to talk.

Although she'd struggled to uphold her end of the conversation, it was obvious that Brad sensed her strained nerves, though he avoided mentioning the fact. Neither one of them talked about the night they'd just spent together, and Anne wondered miserably if he'd already dismissed their lovemaking from his mind.

She'd certainly given him plenty of encouragement. In fact, looking back now, she felt a little ashamed of her eagerness. She couldn't help but wonder if his opinion of her had lessened because of her aggressive behavior last night.

By the time he finally pulled up in front of her apartment building, she'd convinced herself that he no longer respected her, and had relegated her to his list of ex-conquests.

As the car halted she released her seat belt and reached for the door. "Thank you again, Brad, for the great job you did, for the meals, and for my little house. I'll enjoy adding it to my collection."

"Annie."

Already halfway out of the door, she froze.

"Annie, about last night. I—"

Unable to stand hearing him say the words, she

interrupted. "Last night was wonderful, Brad. But it's over now, and we have to go back to our respective lives. I know that. Let's not spoil things by hashing them over, okay?"

His voice sounded odd when he answered her. "Just another one-night stand, I take it."

Deciding it was relief she'd heard, she made herself look at him. "Don't worry, Brad. I won't hold it against you. Thanks for getting my settlement for me. I truly am grateful."

She flung herself out of the door without waiting to hear his answer. The snow-covered pavement was slick under her feet, and she almost fell. Recovering just in time, she headed into her apartment building with one thought in her mind. To get into her apartment and close the door on everything that had happened since she'd left yesterday morning. It seemed a lifetime away now.

She heard the roar of Brad's car as it pulled away from the curb, and spared one fleeting wish that he would take care driving back to his house. Then she let herself into the lonely security of her living room.

There was a message on her phone from her mother, who'd called the night before demanding to know where she was.

Deciding to ignore it, Anne made some hot tea and took the cup with her into the bedroom, where she peeled off the clothes she'd been wearing since yesterday. Chilled to the bone, she pulled on a soft, warm robe and her fur-lined slippers.

She returned to the living room, just as the phone started ringing. For one wild moment she wondered if it was Brad, calling to let her know he was home, then common sense warned her it was probably her mother. Unable to face the explanations she knew her mother would demand, she sank onto the couch and let the phone ring. Tomorrow, she promised herself. Tomorrow she would face the world again. But right now, she simply wanted to stop thinking about anything and rest her troubled mind.

In the cold light of day, she had to face what she could not accept last night. That whenever she was alone with Brad Irving, her common sense deserted her. She was so in love with him that she found it impossible to resist him.

Last night, with his arms around her and his mouth on hers, she'd lost all concept of values and consequences. She could not go on sneaking around, being disloyal to her family and to herself, knowing that she was fighting a losing battle. She and Brad had no future together. It was time she accepted that, and got on with her own life.

When her mother called the next day, she told her she'd been on a business trip to Denver, without mentioning Brad at all. The next few days seemed to drag by, as she fought the weariness that fogged her mind and depressed her soul. Every time the phone rang she hesitated to answer it, half afraid it could be Brad, and the other half of her afraid it wouldn't be and she'd have to deal with the disappointment.

She wasn't sure what she'd expected. Maybe a call from him to ask about her health. Maybe a follow-up on the settlement case. Maybe even a bill from him for his services. Somehow she hadn't expected total silence from him.

She kept remembering that afternoon in Denver—

the way they'd laughed over that silly hat, the sound of a jazz band on the chilly, snow-covered streets, the look in his eyes when she'd stood with him in his room, offering her body and, although he hadn't known it, her love. It was so hard to believe that it had all meant so little to him, he could put it out of his mind completely and never look back.

Exactly a week after her trip to Denver, her mother called the office. Anne knew, the moment she picked up the phone, that something was wrong. Her mother's usual clipped tone was high-pitched and close to hysterical.

"Is it Daddy?" Anne asked fearfully, certain that her father had suffered the heart attack everyone kept predicting.

"Your father is fine," her mother said, her voice cracking on the last word. "It's you I'm concerned about."

"Me?" For a crazy moment she thought her mother knew about her pregnancy. But that was impossible. "Why are you worried about me?"

There was a long pause on the phone that seemed far more ominous than anything her mother could have said. Finally, her mother replied, sounding a little more calm. "This afternoon I received a piece of your mail. Apparently you still have our address on your credit card account. I opened it, thinking it was for me. It was from the Preston Hotel in Denver. A receipt for two rooms, with an extra charge for room service. You must have checked out without paying for your breakfast for two."

Anne sighed. "The charge probably hadn't gone through when they made out the receipt."

Her mother's voice turned accusing. "You didn't tell me you spent the night in Denver."

"It was snowing, and the roads were—"

"You were with that man."

Anne closed her eyes. More lies. More evasions. What a fool she'd been. "Brad was acting as my attorney in the settlement case. I told you that. We intended to come back after the meeting, but then the snowstorm hit—"

"How convenient."

Resentment flared, despite her best efforts to prevent it. "Mother, I'm old enough and certainly capable enough of living my own life without you telling me how I should live it."

"Really. It doesn't matter at all to you that people will talk? That your father will find out? Do you have any idea what that will do to him, to know that you and that man spent the night together at a hotel?"

"I think it's a little late to worry about that, considering we already spent two nights together in an isolated cabin in the mountains."

"That was unavoidable," Carol Parker said sharply. "Besides, you told me nothing happened. This was deliberate. How could you, Anne?"

"Mother, if you look at the receipt you'll see I paid for two rooms. Two separate rooms."

"And you had breakfast together in one of them."

"For convenience. We were in a hurry to leave. What was I supposed to do? Insist on eating breakfast alone in my room? Isn't that a little childish?"

She heard her mother's uncertainty when she answered, and hated herself for the deception. Although she hadn't exactly lied this time, she hadn't told the truth, either. This had to be the last time. She just couldn't go on deceiving her family like this. Tomorrow she would tell them and face the music.

She stayed home the next day, rehearsing over and over the words that would destroy her family's faith in her. She hoped it wouldn't destroy their love and compassion. She was going to need them all in the months and years ahead.

That evening, feeling more sick than she ever remembered, she drove the slushy roads to her parents' house. She would not let herself think beyond the next few hours. Each day would be tough enough to face. Right now all she could do was get through one ordeal at a time.

Paul opened the door to her knock, and seemed surprised to see her. "They're in the family room watching TV," he told her, when she asked about her parents. "So what's up? Not going back to Denver, are you?"

She sent him a startled glance. "Of course not. What made you say that?"

Paul shrugged. "Oh, I don't know. Mom's been moping around a bit these last few days. She won't say what's wrong. I just thought maybe you were leaving town again. She was real upset the last time you went."

"I know," Anne said, feeling guilty. "But I'm not leaving town."

"Good. See you later then." He clattered up the

stairs and disappeared around the corner, heading for his room.

Anne braced herself and opened the door to the family room. Her mother looked up at once, her face breaking out into a pleased smile. "Anne! We were wondering when you'd get around to visiting us. It seems ages since we've seen you."

The guilt intensified. "I know, I'm sorry." She walked over to her father and dropped a kiss on his cheek. "I've just been so busy. How are you doing, Daddy?"

"Better now you're here." He patted the spot on the couch next to him. "Come and sit down and tell me what you've been doing lately."

Anne's mother cleared her throat and gave an almost imperceptible shake of her head that Anne interpreted immediately. Apparently her mother hadn't said anything to her father about her trip to Denver. Not that it mattered now, in view of what she was about to tell them.

She glanced at the TV. "I don't want to interrupt your show."

"Oh, we're not really watching it." Her father reached for the remote and snapped off the picture. "So what have you been up to?"

"Not a lot. I'm still trying to set up some appointments with prospective clients, but I really don't have anything finalized yet."

He gave her a close look. "Not worrying about it, are you? You'll get something soon. It takes time to establish a new business. Meanwhile, if you need money…"

She shook her head. "Thanks, Dad, but I have my

settlement from the Stewarts, and that will more than tide me over until I get going.''

''Okay. Just let me know if you find yourself short of cash.''

''Would you like a drink?'' Carol asked, beginning to get up. ''I was thinking of getting myself a cup of cocoa.''

''Not right now.'' She could feel her stomach muscles tightening, and knew if she didn't get it out now, she would never find the nerve. ''Mom, sit down. There's something I have to tell you.''

Her mother's face grew instantly wary. She sat down slowly, as if bracing herself for something terrible.

For a fleeting moment Anne wondered if it might not have been better to tell her mother on her own, so that she could tell her husband later, but in the next instant she knew she was just being a coward. She had to face them now, together. They both deserved to know the truth. To know what a stupid, irresponsible thing she had done.

Swallowing hard, she looked at her parents' expectant faces and prepared to deliver the blow.

Chapter 13

The silence in the room grew more foreboding as Anne sought for the right words, to drop the bombshell. There were no right words, of course. No soft phrases or gentle explanations. There was only the truth. And it was time to tell them the truth.

"I want you to let me finish before you say anything," she began. "Can you do that for me?"

Her mother's hand fluttered to her throat, while her father looked grim. "You're in trouble," he said gruffly. "I told you I could help out."

"You can't help me with this." Unexpectedly she felt tears threatening, and struggled for a moment to contain them.

"Anne...whatever it is..." Her mother's voice faded away as Anne shook her head.

"No, let me tell you. Then you can have your say. Okay?"

"Go ahead."

Her father suddenly looked older, and Anne felt a chill of fear. If anything happened to him because of what she'd done... "Daddy, I'm sorry. You, too, Mom. The truth is, I'm...pregnant. I've thought about this, and I'm not prepared to marry the father of my child. I intend to keep the baby and bring it up by myself. I know this must be a great shock for you, and I'm so sorry."

The silence went on and on, while both her parents stared at her in disbelief. Now that she had the floor, there didn't seem to be anything else to say.

"Thank God," her father said at last. "I thought you were going to tell us you had an incurable disease."

Anne shot a look at her mother, who was staring at her white-faced. It was obvious she had already guessed what her father only now was working out in his mind.

"Wait a minute," he said harshly. "Who—? No. It can't be. Why that s—"

"Daddy!" Anne said sharply. "You can't blame Brad. It was...mutual. I'm a big girl. I knew what I was doing."

"Obviously you didn't," her mother said brokenly. "I can't believe you and that man—"

"Would you please stop calling him that man. His name is Brad."

"Bradley Irving," her father said, sounding dazed.

"He'll have to marry you, of course," her mother put in.

Dan Parker made a choking sound, then roared, "Dammit, Carol! Bradley Irving?"

Her mother let out a loud wail. "What am I saying? A Parker can't marry an Irving."

"Not again," her father said grimly. "Not ever again."

"Will you both please be quiet and listen to me!"

Anne's sharp command finally penetrated, and her father subsided onto his chair while her mother fished in her pocket for a tissue and blew her nose.

"Now," Anne said more quietly, "this is hard enough for me without you both making such a fuss. No one said anything about me marrying Brad. As I've said, I've already decided that would not be a good idea. Everything will be fine. Single women have babies every day. I'll manage. I have a good career that allows me to work at home if I choose. There's no reason why I can't raise a baby on my own." She looked at her mother. "Right now I could use some understanding and support."

Her mother sniffed, wiped her nose, then said tearfully, "My first grandchild. How could you? What am I going to tell the girls, and Paul?"

"An Irving. You can't be serious," Dan Parker groaned.

"Not an Irving," Anne insisted. "My baby will grow up a Parker. And as long as I'm part of this family, you will all accept this child as one of us."

Carol glanced across the room at her husband. "It would be nice to have a baby in the family again."

Dan Parker grunted. "It will have Irving blood, Carol."

Having taken as much as she could manage, Anne got to her feet. All she could hope for was that once her mother got used to the idea, she'd persuade her husband to accept what could not be changed.

Now, all that remained was to give Brad the news. And that was something she was dreading with every fiber of her being.

The snow had started falling again the next morning when Anne left for the office. She'd call him first, she decided as she parked in front of the curb. Barging into his office on the off chance he'd be there alone didn't seem like a good idea. He could be with a client. Out on a case somewhere. She needed to set this up, so that she'd only have to brace herself for the ordeal once. And once was more than enough.

He answered the phone on the first ring. She hadn't really expected him to be there. She certainly hadn't expected him to answer the phone himself. Taken completely by surprise, she stuttered, "W-where's Rita?"

"Flu," Brad said, sounding wary. "Is something up? The settlement went through all right, didn't it?"

"Well, I haven't received the check yet, but I did get a confirmation in the mail, so I imagine it will arrive soon."

"Well, let me know if you don't get it in a couple of weeks."

"I will." She'd rehearsed the scene so often in her mind, yet now that she could put it off no longer, nothing that she'd intended to say seemed appropriate. She paused, all her carefully prepared words vanishing like mist from her mind.

"So why did you call?"

She fixed her gaze on her wall clock, watching the

second hand swing smoothly down one side and up the other. "Could you meet me for lunch?"

The significant pause that followed betrayed his surprise. "Er...today?"

"Preferably, if you could manage it."

"Well, let me see."

She waited, trying to subdue the thunderous thumping of her heart, while he apparently checked his calendar. "I think I can make it by one-thirty," he said at last. "Is that too late for you?"

"One-thirty's fine. Where?"

"How about the diner?"

"Fine. I'll meet you there."

"Annie?"

She paused in the act of removing the receiver from her ear. "Yes?"

"I have the feeling this isn't a purely social invitation. Want to give me a clue what it's all about?"

"I'll tell you when I see you." She put down the phone before he could ask any more questions.

Ten minutes later, in the middle of sketching out a new Web page, it occurred to her that the diner might not be the best place to blurt out her news. She reached for the phone and dialed Brad's number, only to hear his recorded voice suggesting she leave her number.

Frowning, she replaced the receiver. He might check his messages before he went to the diner. Then again, he might not. She didn't have the number of his cell phone. There didn't seem to be any option but to go to the diner and meet him there.

She spent the rest of the morning in an adrenalin-induced haze. How did one tell a man that she was having his baby? It was the kind of thing younger adults did. Not grown, sensible career women who should know better. How had she let this happen? How had *he* let this happen? How could she allow a few stolen moments to totally change her whole life?

By the time she got into her car to drive to the diner, her hands shook so badly she could hardly hold the wheel steady. Her stomach growled in anticipation of being fed, yet she was certain she wouldn't get a single mouthful down.

There were several cars parked outside the building, but Brad's was not among them. She didn't know whether to be thankful or dismayed about that. Luckily a corner table was vacant, and she slunk onto her seat, feeling as if every eye in the place was scrutinizing her.

Hiding behind the large, plastic-coated menu, she tried not to notice it shaking as she studied the items listed. Nothing seemed appetizing, and she decided to play it safe and order a salad. Several people got up and left while she waited, until only she and an elderly couple were still seated in the corner.

The waitress approached, pad in one hand, pen in the other. Anne knew her vaguely by sight, having visited the diner a few times when she was home. She smiled in recognition and the waitress grinned back. "All alone today?"

"No, I'm meeting someone," Anne began.

Then her stomach dropped when a deep voice added, "And I'm late. My apologies." He slid into the seat opposite her. "Got held up at a meeting. Have you been here long?"

"Only a few minutes," Anne told him, glancing at

her watch. She was telling the truth, though to her it had felt like hours since she'd walked into the place.

"I'll come back when you've decided," the waitress said, flashing a toothy smile at Brad.

He barely acknowledged her. "You don't look well, Annie. Are you all right?"

She pressed her lips together, torn with indecision. Did she tell him now, and ruin his appetite, or struggle through lunch and wait until she could escape right after she gave him the news?

His look of concern deepened. "Annie? Are you going to tell me what's wrong, or do I have to drag it out of you word by word?"

"I've had a touch of the flu," she said, deciding to wait until later. "But I'm over it now."

"I'm sorry." He narrowed his eyes, as if unconvinced. "Did you go to the doctor?"

She shook her head. "No, but I will if it doesn't go away soon." God, listen to her. She was getting so good at lying even she half believed what she said.

"So, what was it you wanted to tell me?"

She made herself smile at him. "Lunch first. I imagine you're hungry by now." She looked around for the waitress, who came hurrying over as soon as she caught her eye.

"I'll have the chicken Caesar salad," she told the girl, "and an iced tea."

"Steak sandwich," Brad ordered. "And coffee."

"Fries?" The waitress flapped her eyelashes at him.

"No fries."

The waitress scurried away and Brad leaned back in his chair. "So, how's the business going?"

"Slow." She glanced out of the window. "This isn't a good time of the year to hire an architect."

"What does an architect do when she's not busy?"

She kept her gaze on the snowy scene outside. It was painful to look at him. Every time she saw him he seemed more appealing. Her Viking. Tall and blond and striking. She wondered if their baby would resemble him, and caught back the thought before it became too painful. "Hunt for prospects, design Web pages, work on pet projects that will probably never materialize."

"What's your pet project?"

She found the strength to meet his gaze. "An office complex, with a restaurant on the top floor and a small arcade of shops."

"For Grand Springs?"

"You don't think there's a place for one here?"

"I don't know...I guess." He laughed, a rich sound that seemed to reverberate all the way down her spine. "I don't know how great the demand is for office space, though Grand Springs is growing fast. I daresay there will be a need sooner or later."

"That's what I think." Feeling safer now that she was on familiar territory, she launched into an enthusiastic description of her vision for the offices.

The waitress brought the food before she was done, and she realized she'd been prattling on without giving Brad a chance to comment. "I'm sorry," she said, when the waitress left them alone again. "I get carried away when it comes to work."

"So I've noticed." He picked up his sandwich and took a chunk out of it. "That's why I'm surprised you left Denver to come back here," he added, when he could talk again. "Aren't you giving up a lot of opportunities by coming back to a small town like Grand Springs?"

She shrugged. "Perhaps. Who knows? At the time it felt like a good idea, and so far I've had no reason to regret it."

He studied her for a minute before taking another bite. "You must have been pretty shattered to give up everything. It couldn't have been easy to build up your name in a city that size."

"It wasn't and I was," she said quietly. "Shattered, I mean. It wasn't so much that Jason betrayed me. It was the fact that he'd cheated on me with someone I'd considered a very good friend. That hurt."

"I imagine it did." His dark gaze probed her face. "Betrayal is never easy to deal with."

"I should have known. Somehow I think I always did know, deep in my mind, that Jason couldn't be trusted. He lied too easily, for too little reason. He embarrassed me. I was sure people couldn't possibly believe some of the wild tales he made up. The worst part about it was it didn't seem to bother him that I knew he was lying."

"Well, we all make mistakes. The important thing is not to let them hold you back. You have to put them behind you and get on with your life."

Anne picked at her salad with her fork. How was she supposed to do that, when the consequences of her mistake, *their* mistake, would be a very big part of the rest of her life?

Brad must have sensed her disquiet. He put down his coffee mug and leaned forward. "Annie, isn't it time you told me why you wanted to see me?"

Out of the corner of her eye, she saw the elderly couple get up slowly from the table. She waited while the man helped his wife on with her coat, then watched him pick up the bill and shuffle up the aisle to the cash register.

The woman took longer, fiddling with her umbrella, dragging on her gloves, fussing with her handbag, until finally she trudged up the aisle to join her husband.

Left alone with Brad in the isolated corner of the diner, Anne sought for the words, then decided there was only one way to tell him. Lowering her voice, she whispered, "I'm pregnant."

She couldn't look at him. She knew by his stunned silence he'd heard her. She just kept her gaze fixed on the couple at the counter, watching them until the little man opened the door for his wife and they disappeared outside.

"How long have you known?"

She took one, quick glance at his white face, then transferred her gaze back to the window. "Officially, about a week."

"And you didn't tell me? You've been to a doctor?"

"I used an H.P.T."

"What—?"

"Home pregnancy test."

"Is it reliable?"

"As reliable as it gets."

"I see." He barely paused. "So when do you want to get married?"

It took her a moment or two to get her breath. She felt as if someone had punched her in the stomach. "This isn't a laughing matter."

"I'm serious, Annie. You didn't think I'd let you handle this alone, did you?"

She risked a fleeting glance. He looked perfectly composed, without a trace of concern in his dark blue eyes. "Thank you, but I really don't think we need to compound one big mistake with another even bigger one."

"Mistake?"

Reaching the limit her composure could take her, she snapped. Leaning forward, she muttered, "What the hell do you call it, Brad? A misfired joke? For once in your life, be serious and think about the consequences. A baby. A human life. And I'm responsible."

"*We're* responsible. I want to marry you, Annie. I know this isn't the most romantic proposal—"

"No!" The word was wrung from her heart. The pain of hearing him say the words almost destroyed her. Such empty words for him, and so agonizingly bittersweet to her ears. "I can't marry you, Brad. Even if I thought you were sincere."

"Dammit, Annie, I *am* sincere." He reached out and grasped her arm. "Why are you fighting me on this?"

She pulled free from him and pushed her chair

back. "I won't trap you into being somewhere you don't want to be. You said yourself, that's no way to find happiness. Thank you, Brad, but I've made up my mind. You will have visiting rights, but I will rear this child alone."

"As a Parker?"

She stared into his eyes, and for the first time since that day he'd walked away from her in the school-yard, she saw white-hot anger there. "Yes," she said quietly. "As a Parker."

His mouth thinned. "Over my dead body."

Once Brad Irving's temper was aroused, she was beginning to realize, he was a formidable enemy. Undaunted, she rose to her feet. "Do what you like, Brad, but this is one time you will not get your way. You had better accept that. This is my baby, and neither you, nor your insufferable mother can take it away from me. Try, and I promise you, the Parkers will bring the gates of hell down on your head."

Her knees trembled as she made her way to the door. She half expected him to come after her, and was prepared to battle him tooth and nail, but the door closed behind her and she made it to the car without hearing her name called or the touch of his hand on her shoulder.

Once she was safely inside her car, she let the trembling take over. She should be gratified that he offered to marry her. Maybe she would have been if this hadn't turned into a battle for the defenseless child inside her.

She felt cold, and immeasurably miserable. And

scared to death. Brad was a lawyer, and a good one. She had a tough fight on her hands.

She put her hands on the wheel to stop them from shaking. She was the mother. Mothers generally got custody unless someone showed good reason why she would be unfit to be a mother. She had a good job, or she would have, when she got some business going. The chill of fear almost choked her. She had to find some customers soon. If she didn't she wouldn't be able to prove she was self-sufficient.

Damn, why did this all have to be so complicated? Why couldn't Brad be the kind of man she could trust to settle down and enjoy bringing up a family? Why couldn't he just let her be to deal with this as she felt best?

Without warning the door on her left opened. "Move over," Brad commanded.

She stared at his rigid face. "Go away," she said brokenly. "I don't want to talk to you."

"You have to talk to me sometime. We have to settle this."

"Not now."

"Now is as good a time as any. Move over."

Instead of moving, she fitted the key in the ignition and turned it. The engine leapt to life, and she slid the lever into gear. "I'm sorry, Brad, but I don't feel like talking now. I'll set up a meeting with Mark Peterson and let you know where and when."

"Annie—"

"Goodbye, Brad." She released the brake and let the car roll forward.

For an instant she thought he was going to leap

into the car, but with a look of defeat on his face she knew she'd never forget, he slammed the door and stood back.

Tears spurted from her eyes as she pulled onto the highway, and she dashed them away with the back of her hand. It was done. From now on she'd let Mark handle matters. As far as she and Brad were concerned, there was nothing more to say.

Chapter 14

Anne didn't go back to the office that afternoon. There didn't seem to be any point. There were no deadlines, no urgent meetings, no arrangements to take care of, no phone calls to make.

Instead, she drove to the park, and walked the frosted paths between bare-limbed trees and snow-covered grass. Robins and sparrows hopped behind her, hoping to spot a crumb or two in her wake. She wished she'd brought the remains of the bread roll she'd left on her plate. Next time, she promised herself, she'd bring food for the birds.

In spite of her heavy coat and boots she felt cold, inside and out. Her future seemed to stretch ahead of her, confusing and frightening in its uncertainty. Never had she felt more dependent on her family. Never had she been more convinced that it would be a mistake to surrender to that need.

She had left once before, because she'd felt stifled by the constant vigilance on her personal life. It wasn't because her parents didn't care about her. It was because they cared too much.

She'd be wrong to deny Brad his child. Deep down she knew that. Just as it would be wrong to deny the child his father. Or *her* father. Her heart twisted in pain at the mental vision of Brad with a small daughter.

How could she bring up a child torn between two families? How could she make that child understand? How could she be happy herself, forced to stay in contact with the man she loved, knowing there could never be a future between them? So many unanswered questions.

She reached the gate of the park and hurried out to her car. She was so cold, and the ache under her ribs wouldn't go away. She needed to go home, to her empty apartment, and try to work out what seemed to be insurmountable problems. This was one time when she couldn't run to her family for advice or sympathy. She was on her own. And so incredibly lonely.

Once inside her apartment, she filled the bathtub with hot water and soaked her skin until it glowed. Wrapping herself in her thick, white robe, she padded on bare feet to the kitchen and plugged in the coffeepot. There was nothing on television worth watching, and she sorted through a pile of magazines, trying to find one she hadn't already read from cover to cover.

She had reached the last one when the shrill peal of her doorbell startled her. It was probably her mother. Right now she was in no mood to talk to anyone. She stood, undecided, the magazine still in her hand, until the bell rang again.

There seemed no other choice but to answer it. Her car was outside in the parking lot. Her mother would only panic if she didn't open the door.

Bracing herself, she pulled the door open, and stared in astonishment at a young woman holding the largest bouquet of red roses she'd ever seen.

"Ms. Parker?" The woman thrust the flowers at her. "These are for you."

She took the fragrant mass of blossoms in her arms, her head spinning with unspoken questions. Mumbling her thanks, she closed the door and stumbled to the coffee table where she lay the fragile blooms down. Her fingers trembled as she withdrew the card from its tiny envelope.

I don't know what it's going to take to convince you I'm serious, the card read, *but this seemed like a good start. Brad.*

She sank down on the couch, the card pinched between her fingers. Damn him. Didn't he know how much it hurt to dangle empty promises in front of her?

Unable to bring herself to throw the roses away, she put them in water, then sat them in the bathroom so she couldn't stare at them all evening. She went to bed early, determined to make a concerted effort to drum up some business by the end of the week.

Dreams disturbed her sleep—busy, complicated dreams that made no sense. She woke the next morning, feeling the usual spasms of nausea, and dragged herself to the office, although it was the last place she wanted to be.

Her mother called that morning, to tell her that her

father was still in shock at finding out that his first grandchild was fathered by an Irving. "Dan thinks it might be a good idea if you moved back to Denver."

Anne closed her eyes. "Why? Why would he want me to leave Grand Springs?"

"Your father thinks it would be better for everyone."

"And what do *you* think?"

"Well, really, Anne, surely you don't want to risk running into that man every day? It's going to be awkward enough as it is. I can't imagine what his mother is saying about it. The news is probably all over town by now. We'll be the laughingstock of Grand Springs. Imagine, a Parker being the mother of an Irving offspring."

"Can't you and Dad forget about the damned feud for once?" Anne snapped. "There's more to this than a silly argument over land. This is a brand-new child being born into this family. Your grandchild. Surely you can put the past behind you and accept my baby as your own flesh and blood? Is that really too much to ask?"

"You don't understand, Anne. This has been going on for generations. Much as I love the idea of seeing my first grandchild, we can't just dismiss everything because you made a mistake."

"Then you'll just have to accept the fact that as long as my baby is alive, he or she will have contact with Bradley Irving. Like it or not, Mother, *that man* is in our lives to stay."

"It might be easier on everyone if you didn't both live in the same town."

Her mother could be incredibly stubborn. And

cruel. Though Anne had no doubt that her father's convictions were behind her mother's attitude. "Forget it," she said crisply. "I'm not moving to Denver. End of discussion."

She hung up, and buried her head in her hands. She would not run away. Not again. Not ever again.

The flowers kept coming, every day. They came to the office, they came to her apartment, and once she walked out to her car to find it festooned with roses. Always the cards said the same. *I'm serious, Annie. Marry me.*

She walked the park every afternoon, in the wind, in the snow and sometimes in brilliant sunshine, trying to analyze her own feelings. Was she refusing Brad's offer because of fear of trapping him into something he didn't want, or was she once more letting her family influence her decision?

How could she trust him, knowing how he felt about marriage? How could she marry a man, never knowing if he loved her, or if he'd married her because he felt obligated? Surely those were legitimate concerns? Yet still the haunting feeling nagged her that, just maybe, she was afraid to add more complications to an already complex situation. Maybe, deep down, the old values of family loyalty were stronger than her own convictions.

If only she could be sure of Brad's true motivations in asking her to marry him. She could still remember his anger the day she told him she would raise the child on her own. If only she could feel that it was a little more than simply a desire to see his child raised as an Irving.

In all the time they'd been together, she'd never

heard him say the words that might have helped her make up her mind. Never once had he told her he loved her.

She came home one afternoon from the office to find yet another bouquet of roses waiting on her doorstep. This time there were different words written on the card. This time the card read, *I'm taking you somewhere special for dinner tonight. Be ready at seven. Brad.*

Feverishly she lunged for the phone, determined to put an end to this ridiculous and fruitless campaign. Silence hadn't helped. It was time to tell—to demand—that Bradley Irving stop hounding her and leave her alone.

Rita answered the phone and informed her that Brad had left the office and would be out of touch until after the weekend. Frustrated, Anne replaced the receiver. High-handed tactics were not going to work, she promised herself. She simply wouldn't open the door when he arrived.

She waited, heart pounding, for the doorbell to ring that evening. When it came, her knees buckled, and she had to grab the edge of the kitchen counter for support. Somehow she had to find the strength to get rid of him. She had to find the right words that would send him out of her life, at least emotionally, forever.

She'd purposefully dressed in jeans and a pink sweater, determined that he would not persuade her to change her mind. When she opened the door, the first sight of him rocketed her pulse, and she fought for breath.

He wore jeans, too. His parka was the same one he'd worn on the mountain. So was the black sweater.

For the first time since they'd been rescued, he looked like the man who'd stolen her heart, in a shabby, rickety old shack on the slopes of a storm-swept mountain.

"I see you're ready," he said, skimming his gaze up and down her body. "Good. Grab your coat and let's go."

"I'm not going anywhere with you, Brad."

He smiled, and leaned one hand on the doorjamb, bringing his face in close to hers. "Oh, didn't I tell you? This isn't an invitation. It's a command."

She jerked back as if she'd been stung. "No one, not even you, can tell me what to do anymore. Go away, Brad. You and I have nothing more to say to each other."

He tilted his head back and sighed. "I was afraid you were going to take that attitude. Which is why I formulated Plan B."

"It won't make any difference how many plans you formulate." She grabbed the door and started to close it. "Goodbye, Brad."

To her dismay he blocked the door open with his foot. "You don't get it, Annie. You're coming with me, willingly or not."

Close to breaking point, she gritted her teeth. "And who's going to make me?"

"I am." Before she could react he stepped inside her living room, and bodily picked her up in his arms. "Now," he said calmly, "you could, of course, fight me, but I'm stronger than you. You could scream and yell, but that would bring your neighbors running, and I don't think your parents would take too kindly to the gossip that is bound to circulate. The third alternative is to go quietly, and at least give me a chance to show you something that I think will be of great interest to you.''

Why, she thought miserably, did her insides melt every time he touched her? Why couldn't she look into his intense blue eyes without remembering the fire in them when he made love to her? Why, even now, did her mind scream at her to forget everything except the one, burning conviction that her heart was his and could never belong to another?

She didn't struggle. She didn't react at all.

After a moment he set her on her feet, and for the first time since she'd known him, she saw fear in his eyes. The knowledge gave her a spark of hope.

"So," he said quietly, "what's it going to be? Will you come willingly or not?"

"Where are we going?"

"I'd rather not say until we get there."

It was that look in his eyes that decided her. "All right. I'll get my jacket."

His grin transformed his face, and as she climbed into the passenger seat of his car, she wondered if she was making the biggest mistake of her life.

"I've got to stop by my place," he said, as they turned onto Highway 93.

She glanced at him in surprise. "This isn't the way to your house."

"I know. I want to show you something first."

Her heart lurched against her ribs. "What is it?"

"You'll see."

"You're being very mysterious."

"I want to surprise you."

"You've always been very good at doing that."

He smiled. "I hope so. This is very important to me. I hope to us. You might say, everything depends on you liking what you see."

She stirred in her seat, uncomfortable now. She should never have come with him. He was getting the wrong idea, and she'd tried so hard to make him understand. There could be no cozy relationship between them. That would just be too hard to bear.

When he pulled onto the freeway she began to get nervous. "How far are we going? I don't want to be out too late. I have an appointment in the morning." She didn't, but now that she was with him, all she could think about was putting an end to the agony as quickly as possible.

"Not far now." The car turned sharply, jolting her against his arm. She pulled back, her apology dying on her lips. After a moment she said in disbelief, "We're going to Coldwater?"

He gave her a brief nod. "More or less."

She sank back, her hands clenched in her lap. The damn land. The core of this whole miserable problem. Why would he bring her here now, of all times? Why—? Her thoughts broke off abruptly as the headlights swept the road ahead of them.

She sat up, peering out of the window in disbelief. In spite of the dark night, the lights of town lit up the sky, reflected back to earth by the heavy clouds. She could see the distinctive skyline of Grand Springs, and the ridge of mountains beyond. What she couldn't see was the towering main building, or the long, two-story structures that housed the guest rooms of Coldwater Spa. In fact, all she could see was bare land, stretching out toward the city like a massive plowed field.

When she had finally convinced herself that she wasn't seeing things, she turned back to Brad, who was watching her with a cautious expression that betrayed his apprehension. "It's gone," she said, still unable to fully believe it. "You've torn down the spa."

"I'm surprised you hadn't heard already. The news is all over town."

"I haven't talked to anyone except my mother." And she'd be the last one to mention it, she thought wryly.

"Ah, then it's an even bigger surprise than I planned." He opened the car door and swung his legs out. "Come on, I want to show you."

"Show me what?" She waved a hand at the windshield. "There's nothing to see but bare land."

He climbed all the way out then poked his head inside. "For once in your life, would you do something without arguing about it first? Just trust me, okay?"

Trust him. If only she could. Sighing, she scrambled out her side of the car and pulled her jacket collar up over her ears. "If you think I'm going to tramp through all that mud with you, you're in for a big disappointment."

"No tramping, I promise. Come here." He grabbed her hand and pulled her to what remained of the grand entrance that had once been a popular resort.

Standing with him in the dark, she felt the chill of the wind blowing across the desolate space, and shivered. He pulled her close to him and put his arm around her. Somehow she couldn't find the strength to pull away.

"Look out there," he said, pointing in the direction of the city. "What do you see?"

She frowned. "The lights of Grand Springs."

"How far do you think we are from town?"

"About fifteen miles, I guess."

"Good guess. It's a little under fourteen."

She looked up at him. "When are you going to get to the point?"

Expecting a smart answer, she was taken aback by the gravity of his expression when he answered her. "Would you say that was close enough to town to commute comfortably from here?"

"You're going to build a house out here?" Had he brought her all the way out here to bribe her with the promise of a new house? Didn't he know there was a lot more to it than that? Didn't he understand anything she'd said?

"Not a house. Lots of houses. An entire community. Subsidized housing for low-income families. It's badly needed in this area. Grand Springs has one of the highest priced housing communities in the country. I've talked to the city council, the county commissioners and the governor. They're all willing to back me on this."

Impressed, she stared up at him. "Brad, that's wonderful. But—"

He kissed his finger and laid it on her lips. "Wait, let me finish. I want this to be a joint venture. I'll deed half the land over to your family, if you'll agree to design the development, and your father will agree to build the houses. It will be drawn up as a partnership. Joint ownership between the Parkers and the Irvings. What do you think?''

It was an incredibly generous offer. Not only in monetary value, but in the goodwill that went with it. After everything her parents had said about his family, and him in particular, she could only imagine what this decision was costing him in pride.

''I think you're out of your mind,'' she said unsteadily. ''Wasn't it your father's wish that the land remain in the Irving family? No matter how you feel about it, you can't go against his wishes.''

''Ah, well, that's where this last bit comes in.'' He turned her in his arm and pulled her close to his chest. ''If you marry me, Annie Parker, you and your family will be my family.''

She could feel tears stinging her eyes. He had done this for her. He had given her an answer to her biggest problem. A way out. If she married him. But there was still her doubts to deal with, and they wouldn't be so easily resolved. ''Brad, I can't marry you knowing how you feel about marriage. I—''

This time he cut off her words with his mouth. She was breathless when he finally raised his head. ''You know,'' he said softly, ''you really will have to curb that tendency to argue with me over everything. I know I said a lot of stuff about marriage, but after watching my parents live so miserably together I guess I've been skeptical about the happy-ever-after kind of love.''

''That's the only true kind there is.''

''I know that now.'' The look on his face started her heart thundering again. ''The truth is, Annie, the reason I've never been interested in marriage until now is because I've never met anyone I've really loved. How could I, when I've been in love with the same woman most of my life?"

She could hardly breathe now, terrified she had misunderstood. "What are you saying?"

He hugged her tighter. "Annie, I fell in love with you the day you rammed into me in the schoolyard of Pike Elementary. I took one look at those sad green eyes and trembling mouth, and I was lost. Then, and forever. No woman has ever come close to stealing my heart the way you did that day. You've always been the one, Annie. I just didn't realize it until that night in the cabin, when you turned my world upside down. It hasn't been upright since. And it won't be, until you promise me you'll marry me and love me forever, so we can take care of our baby together."

Speechless, she fought for words, while the world seemed to spin around her in a blaze of lights. Before she could find her voice, he bent his head, bringing his mouth close to hers.

"You *do* love me, don't you?" he asked anxiously. "I'm not just taking things for granted?"

Smiling, she wound her arms around his neck and pulled his mouth down to hers. "Ever since that day you knocked me down at Pike Elementary," she whispered against his lips.

"I didn't knock you down. You rammed into me."

"Shut up and kiss me. You always did talk too much."

"Wait, you haven't said you'll marry me."

She drew back, one last doubt still lingering in her mind. "You're sure you're ready to take on a wife *and* a baby?"

"I'm sure."

"We still have to convince our families. What about your mother? What will she say about this?"

His eyes were grave again as he looked down at her. "Would it make a difference?"

"No," she said confidently, and knew it was true. "As long as you love me, and want me and our baby, I can face anything."

"Then let's find out what they have to say about it."

She felt a twinge of apprehension. "Now?"

"Tomorrow. Tonight I want to seal that promise with a night of unbridled passion."

Relieved, she snuggled close to him. "What about dinner?"

"I'll take care of that, too. At my place."

"You can cook?"

"Of course I can cook. I've lived alone long enough to learn how."

"I wish I'd known that." She tucked her arm in his and drew him back to the car. "I'd have accepted your proposal a lot sooner. By the way, do you have a name for the new development?"

"You bet I do." He opened the car door and waited for her to climb in. "I think it should be called Irving Park."

She was still laughing when they pulled back onto the freeway. That was one of the things she loved best about him. His ability to make her laugh. They still had some bridges to cross, as far as their families were concerned, and they wouldn't be easy, but knowing they'd cross them together made it easier. As long as they kept the laughter in their marriage, they would have that elusive happy-ever-after kind of love. What more could a woman ask?

Epilogue

Although Brad offered to let Anne go alone to talk to her parents the next morning, she insisted on him going with her.

"They might not listen to you," he warned her. "Things could get very uncomfortable. It might be better if you tackled them alone."

She looked at him across the table in his comfortable dining room. They had showered together, and he'd given her a thick, dark green robe to wear. His own navy-blue robe gaped open at his chest and his hair, still damp from the shower, was beginning to curl at the edges. He looked endearingly content, and she felt a tug of tenderness so strong she could hardly breathe.

They had made love again the night before and slept in each other's arms. She'd woken up to a new life, a wonderful new future to share with a husband

and a baby. A whole new world. Nothing, not even the prospect of facing her family, could take away her excitement and joy.

"I'm not marrying my family," she said, reaching for his hand. "I'm marrying you. They can either accept you as my husband, or they can lose their eldest daughter."

"I don't want to be the cause of you losing your family."

"You won't be the cause. They will be." She smiled at him. "Besides, I'm counting on my father's sense of fair play. He's a good man, and he'll realize how generous you are being. He loves me. When he sees how important this is to me, he'll back down."

"And your mother?"

"She wants this grandchild. It will be her first, you know. That's all that will matter to her, you'll see."

He shook his head, and her heart warmed at the pride and wonderment in his eyes. "Wow," he said softly. "Me, a father. Hope I'm up to the challenge."

She laughed. "You'll make a wonderful father. Just don't lose that formidable sense of humor."

"As long as I have you and our children to come home to, I'll always have something to smile about." He glanced up at the ornate clock on the wall. "I guess we should go tell your parents."

"What about your mother?"

"She already knows."

Anne's jaw dropped. "What? Why didn't you tell me? What did she say? You were taking a lot for granted, weren't you? What if I'd turned you down?"

He grinned at her, and raised her fingers to his lips before letting her go. "I told her I was going to ask you to marry me. She was the one who was certain you'd accept.''

"But what about the land? How did she feel about sharing it with the Parkers?''

"Once she found out about the baby, she forgot all about the land. It *is* her first grandchild, too, you know. She shed a few tears, wiped her eyes, then said she never could understand what all the fuss about the land was, anyway. Then she started muttering something about shopping for the baby and that she'd have to call you to see what we needed. By the time I left she was thumbing through catalogues looking for baby clothes.''

Feeling close to tears herself, Anne got up from her chair and walked around the table. Winding her arms around her future husband's neck she whispered, "Isn't it amazing the tremendous power a tiny baby can have?''

"Awesome.'' He pulled her head down and kissed her on the lips. "Now go get dressed. We have a date with your family.''

An hour or so later they pulled up in front of the house that had been home to her for most of her life. In spite of her confident words, Anne felt more than a little apprehensive at the thought of confronting her family. They had to understand. If they couldn't accept Brad's offer, she would have to stand by her husband, and risk losing them altogether. It would be a terrible sacrifice to make, but one she was prepared to accept if the worst happened.

Her mother opened the door, looking a little distraught. "Oh, hello, dear,'' she said, her hand at her throat, "I thought you might be Fiona. Such a terrible thing. Her little girl has been rushed to hospital. Apparently she was hurt in some weird accident. I'm not sure what happened exactly, but Fiona promised to stop by and let me know how Katy was doing—" She broke off, apparently seeing Brad for the first time. Her anxious expression turned to one of resentment, but good manners prevented her from being openly rude to him. Instead, she looked at Anne. "What have you come to tell me?"

"We've come to talk to you both," Anne said, pulling Brad behind her as she stepped into the hallway. "And Grandpa James, too, since this affects him as well."

"I don't see what he has to do with anything," Carol Parker muttered, as she closed the door behind them."

"You will. Where's Daddy?"

"He's in the family room, reading the paper."

"And Gramps?"

"In his room. I really don't think—"

"Please, Mom," Anne pleaded softly. "Just get him."

Carol shot a dark look at Brad, then disappeared up the stairs.

"Come on," Anne said, heading for the living room. "Let's face the lion in his den."

Dan Parker sat in his chair by the fireplace, the newspaper held resolutely in front of his face. Anne knew, by the tight clench of his fingers, that he'd heard their voices and was braced for a confrontation.

Her throat felt constricted, and she cleared it before saying, "Daddy? We've come to talk to you."

For a long moment she thought he was going to ignore them. Brad gave her fingers an encouraging squeeze and she sent him a weak smile. Then her father lowered the paper.

"And what in the world makes you think I'd be interested in anything you have to say?" he demanded, looking straight at Brad. "If you've come to tell me you're marrying my daughter, there's not much I can do about that, except to tell you you're the last person in the world I'd want to see her married to, but then I guess she has no choice."

"Daddy—" Anne began hotly, but Brad gave her a quick shake of his head.

"Mr. Parker," he said quietly. "I'm sorry—very sorry—that it happened this way, but I want you to know I love your daughter very much, and I'll do my very best to take care of her and our baby. I intend to make them both happy. I'm hoping you will be happy for us, too. For Anne's sake."

Dan Parker grunted, and retreated behind the newspaper again.

"Well said, son," a gravelly voice said behind him. "Why the heck didn't someone tell me there was a little one on the way?"

Anne turned and smiled at her grandfather. "Hi, Gramps."

Grandpa James nodded at her, then made his way to his armchair and sat down.

"Would anyone like a cup of coffee?" Carol asked nervously. She hovered in the doorway as if afraid to come any closer to the little group in the room.

"Come and sit down," Anne said, pulling Brad

over to the couch. "We can have coffee later. Brad has something he wants to tell you."

Carol hurried across the room and perched on the arm of her husband's chair. "Anne, I don't want to hurry you—"

"Don't worry, this won't take long." Anne gave Brad's hand a little shake. "Go ahead, Brad. Tell them."

She sat there watching his face while he outlined his plan. After the first few words, Dan lowered the newspaper, and only Brad's voice interrupted the stunned silence in the room. Even Grandpa James sat transfixed, his watery blue gaze fastened on Brad's face while he explained what he wanted to do with the land.

When he stopped talking, everyone sat without saying a word. Looking at their faces, Anne tried to gauge their reactions. Grandpa James looked impressed, her father looked stunned and her mother looked as if she'd opened a gift and found something far beyond her expectations.

"Well, Daddy?" Anne said quietly. "What do you think?"

Dan Parker laid the newspaper down on his lap and shook his head. "I don't know what to think. A partnership? Between the Parkers and the Irvings? They're all going to turn in their graves."

"More than a partnership," Brad said, putting his arm around his future wife's shoulders. "We'll be one family. What better way to end a feud?"

Dan's face darkened. "Now wait a minute—"

"Shut up, Dan," Grandpa James said gruffly. "You always were too damn stubborn for your own good." He got up slowly from his chair and held out his hand to Brad. "That's a pretty generous offer you made there, son. I admire you for it. Welcome to the family."

Brad shook his hand, traces of his grin appearing on his face. "Thank you, sir. It's an honor to be marrying your granddaughter."

"Make sure you never forget that." Grandpa James turned to his son. "Get up off your backside, Dan, and shake this boy's hand. Not only is he giving you a fair share of the land, he's offering you one hell of a deal for your business. And he's marrying your daughter. Dammit, man, you're going to be a grandfather!" He took a step back, clutching his heart. "Goldarnit, that'll make me a great-grandfather."

He looked so comical Anne had to smile. She glanced apprehensively at her father, who was folding his newspaper neatly into a square. Finally, he gave it to Carol and pushed himself to his feet.

"You know, the old man could be right, for once," he said heavily. "I figure any man who has the good sense to fall in love with my daughter and stand by her has to have some decent blood in his veins. I guess I can think of a lot worse people I could have as family." He held out his hand. "Thanks for the offer, Brad. I reckon you've got yourself a deal."

Tears stung her eyes as Anne jumped to her feet and threw her arms around her father. "Thank you, Daddy," she whispered.

"Don't thank me," he said gruffly. "Thank this future husband of yours. He's the only one with any common sense around here."

Carol jumped to her feet. "I'll go put the coffee on," she said, starting across the room.

"Coffee, hell!" Dan Parker roared. "This is a historic moment. I'll get the scotch." He threw his arm around Brad's shoulders. "Come on, boy, let's drink to the end of that damned feud."

"That's the best idea I've heard yet," Grandpa James muttered.

Brad got to his feet and winked at Anne. "Maybe we should call it Park Irving," he murmured, as they followed Dan Parker to his study.

"I think that's a good idea." She smiled up at him. "You're learning."

He dropped a kiss on her nose. "Happy New Year, Annie."

Sighing, she wrapped an arm around his waist and hugged him. "It's going to be such a wonderful year." And all the years after that, she thought happily. The Parkers and the Irvings together. Somehow she had the feeling that her great-grandparents would be very pleased about that.

*   *   *   *   *

Watch for the final
installment of 36 Hours—
Romance is rekindled between
old flames when Fiona Lake reunites
unexpectantly with police detective
Justin Reed, the father of her child in

MY SECRET VALENTINE

by

Marilyn Pappano

Coming to you from
Silhouette Intimate Moments
in January 2001.

And now for a sneak preview of
MY SECRET VALENTINE,
please turn the page.

Chapter 1

"Fiona."

Tension streaked through her body, clenching her muscles and bringing a sick feeling to her stomach. Justin Reed—she knew his voice. It had seduced her, haunted her, taunted her...and then gone silent on her. No *It's over*. No *Goodbye*. No *I don't want you anymore*. Just silence.

Forcing all emotion from her expression, Fiona slowly turned to face Justin. Handsome? Try *incredible*. This close she could see the deep blue of his eyes, the straight line of his nose, the perpetually stubborn set of his jaw.

She could see the resemblance to her beautiful four-year-old daughter, Katy, that she'd conveniently persuaded herself wasn't there.

She thought of all the things she'd promised herself she would say to him if she ever saw him again.

Every sentiment, every accusation, could be condensed into two harsh words—*Damn you*—but she didn't say them. She didn't say anything at all.

He shifted in a manner that should have screamed *He's nervous!* Of course, it didn't. It just seemed natural. Calm. "I wondered if you were going to speak to me."

"Actually, no. Speaking to you makes it harder to keep up the illusion that I'd never met you."

"And you like pretending you never met me."

She smiled coolly. "I'd like it better if I really had never met you, but this is the next best thing."

A faint hint of bitterness came into his eyes, and his mouth formed a thin line. After a moment, he flatly said, "I'm sorry about Golda."

"Everyone here is sorry about Golda." But in some tender place inside, she was touched by his acknowledgment that losing his aunt Golda was a bigger loss to her than him. After all, she'd seen the old lady every day. He'd stayed away for five years.

Because of her? Or because he hadn't cared any more about his aunt than he had about Fiona?

He shifted again, and this time he did look…not quite nervous. Uncomfortable. As if he wasn't at all accustomed to the position he found himself in—the grieving nephew, the polite ex-lover. "I understand your being here has nothing to do with me, but…thank you anyway."

"You're right. Nothing in my life has anything to do with you." Hoping her hand wouldn't tremble, she gestured toward the center of the church. "You should probably get back over there. There are people waiting who actually *want* to talk to you."

With a solemn nod, he turned and walked away, leaving her feeling...edgy. Guilty. Ashamed. She wasn't a rude person, and had never been cruel a day in her life. She could blame it on Justin. She hadn't been a lot of things until she'd met him—easy, foolish, careless, dreamy, gullible, broken-hearted, pregnant. She hadn't been so strong until she'd loved him and lost him. She needed that strength now to get through the next thirty hours.

She needed it desperately.

presents the gripping miniseries

***WHERE TIME IS
OF THE ESSENCE
IN THE SEARCH
FOR TRUE LOVE....***

CINDERELLA FOR A NIGHT—on sale Sept. 2000
by **Susan Mallery** (IM #1029)

A THANKSGIVING TO REMEMBER—on sale Oct. 2000
by **Margaret Watson** (IM #1035)

A VERY...PREGNANT NEW YEAR'S—on sale Dec. 2000
by **Doreen Roberts** (IM #1047)

MY SECRET VALENTINE—on sale Jan. 2001
by **Marilyn Pappano** (IM #1053)

Don't miss an original
Silhouette Christmas anthology
**36 HOURS: THE CHRISTMAS
THAT CHANGED EVERYTHING**
with stories by
Mary Lynn Baxter, Marilyn Pappano, Christine Flynn
On sale November 2000

Available at yor favorite retail outlet.

Where love comes alive™

Visit Silhouette at www.eHarlequin.com   SIM36H

Coming in January 2001 from Silhouette Books...

ChildFinders, Inc.:
AN UNCOMMON HERO

by

MARIE FERRARELLA

the latest installment of this bestselling author's popular miniseries.

The assignment seemed straightforward: track down the woman who had stolen a boy and return him to his father. But ChildFinders, Inc. had been duped, and Ben Underwood soon discovered that nothing about the case was as it seemed. Gina Wassel, the supposed kidnapper, was everything Ben had dreamed of in a woman, and suddenly he had to untangle the truth from the lies—before it was too late.

Available at your favorite retail outlet.

Silhouette®
Where love comes alive™

Visit Silhouette at www.eHarlequin.com   PSCHILD

Silhouette®

INTIMATE MOMENTS™

Those Marrying McBrides!

Linda Turner's unlucky-in-love McBride siblings are back....

At the advanced age of thirty-seven, Nurse Janey McBride has never been kissed—and never been much of anything else, either. So now she was facing a typical adolescent trauma—how to get the new guy in town to notice her.

She wanted someone to teach her about men, while he needed to learn to live again. Well, maybe they could make a deal. But could love be part of the bargain? Don't miss NEVER BEEN KISSED (IM #1051), Linda Turner's next installment in her *Those Marrying McBrides!* miniseries—on sale in January 2001, only from Silhouette Intimate Moments.

Those Marrying McBrides!: The four *single* McBride siblings have always been unlucky in love. But it looks like their luck is about to change....

Still available! If you missed the earlier titles in this exciting miniseries, don't miss this chance to add to your collection.

#1010	THE BEST MAN	$4.50 U.S.☐	$5.25 CAN.☐
#992	A RANCHING MAN	$4.50 U.S.☐	$5.25 CAN.☐

(limited quantities available)

TOTAL AMOUNT	$	
POSTAGE & HANDLING	$	
($1.00 each book, 50¢ each additional book)		
APPLICABLE TAXES*	$	
TOTAL PAYABLE	$	
(check or money order—please do not send cash)		

To order, send the completed form, along with a check or money order for the total above, payable to Silhouette Books, to: **In the U.S.:** 3010 Walden Avenue, P.O. Box 9077, Buffalo, NY 14269-9077; **In Canada:** P.O. Box 636, Fort Erie, Ontario, L2A 5X3.

Name: _____

Address: _____ City: _____

State/Prov.: _____ Zip/Postal Code: _____

Account # (if applicable): _____ 075 CSAS

*New York residents remit applicable sales taxes.
 Canadian residents remit applicable GST and provincial taxes.

Visit Silhouette at www.eHarlequin.com   SIMMCB2

#1 *New York Times* bestselling author

NORA ROBERTS

brings you more of the loyal and loving,
tempestuous and tantalizing Stanislaski family.

Coming in February 2001

The Stanislaski Sisters

Natasha and Rachel

Though raised in the Old World traditions of their
family, fiery Natasha Stanislaski and cool, classy
Rachel Stanislaski are ready for a *new* world of love....

And also available in February 2001 from
Silhouette Special Edition, the newest book in the
heartwarming Stanislaski saga

CONSIDERING KATE

Natasha and Spencer Kimball's daughter Kate turns her
back on old dreams and returns to her hometown, where
she finds the *man* of her dreams.

Available at your favorite retail outlet.

Silhouette®

Where love comes alive™

Visit Silhouette at www.eHarlequin.com   PSSTANSIS

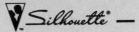
where love comes alive—online...

eHARLEQUIN.com

your romantic escapes

—Indulgences—
♥ Monthly guides to indulging yourself, such as:
  ★ Tub Time: A guide for bathing beauties
  ★ Magic Massages: A treat for tired feet

—Horoscopes—
♥ Find your daily Passionscope, weekly Lovescopes and Erotiscopes

♥ Try our compatibility game

—Reel Love—
♥ Read all the latest romantic movie reviews

—Royal Romance—
♥ Get the latest scoop on your favorite royal romances

—Romantic Travel—
♥ For the most romantic destinations, hotels and travel activities

SINTE1